Blame The G
Vol. 1
In the Beginning There Was Bauhaus.

By Bettina Busiello

Cover Design by Jacob Mathews

Table of Contents

Chapter 1

Onyx

The EMF squealed. There was definitely something here.

… Or it could have been a loose wire. That was the problem with these devices; how unreliable they could be.

"What is it?" Mrs. Sanders asked.

"I'm not sure yet." I looked around and sniffed the air. Another unreliable tool; my sense of smell. Sometimes it was sharp and instant; other times, it was muddled by the scents of those around me. Having Mrs. Sanders in my presence made it more difficult to get a read. "If this place *is* haunted—"

"It is. You have to help me. My daughter refuses to stay with me and it's affecting my custody case." Mrs. Sanders held her hand to her face in worry.

I always hated it when things got too emotional. Why couldn't there be more frat house hauntings? At least there I could get good weed… and a little strange. I sighed. "I can stay the night if you want me to."

She eyed me. I could see the look of desperation overtaking the fact she was seeing a miscreant before her eyes. Jet black hair and thick eye liner framing pale skin might be something people could ignore in passing, but I was in her home— her place of sanctuary. On top of which, I wore my Pennywise the clown shirt for this little gig. Of course my appearance wouldn't help my case… or hers, if she continued with the judgmental looks.

"Listen, I'm not going to take anything. You came to *me* for help, remember?" I turned off the EMF and set it in my duffel bag.

"This is what I do… you can either trust me or judge me. Up to you."

She sighed. "I'm sorry. I didn't mean to—"

"It's okay. I'm used to it." I set my bag down. "It's almost eight. I can stay tonight or come back tomorrow."

"Please, now. It has to be now. The custody hearing is on Monday."

"Alright then." I sat on her daughter's bed. "Guess we're having a slumber party. Got anything to eat?"

She narrowed her eyes at me for a moment before nodding. "Yeah. I can whip up something really fast, I suppose."

****

I set up the motion sensor, temperature gauge, and night vision camera. This was going to be a long night.

Judging by the décor of the daughter's room, she had to be somewhere between ten and twelve. Still young enough to be a little girl's room, but old enough for a girl preparing to enter teenage life. Though the amount of pink was astounding.

After I adjusted the levels on my equipment, I took a better look around. At least she was a fan of Hello Kitty; we could relate there. The flip side of that was, I wasn't very good at talking to children.

There was a knock at the door. "Anything?" Mrs. Sanders asked.

"Not yet. Most paranormal activity either takes place in the dead of night or at a relevant time in which something extreme happened. Take the Alamo for instance: a lot of the action took place during the day, so stories throughout the years say many of the ghosts are spotted in broad daylight."

"I see." She didn't look to be one for a history lesson.

I chewed on the inside of my lower lip, in an effort to search my mind for ideas on keeping the information flowing. "Do you notice any activity when your daughter isn't around?"

"Yes. I'll occasionally hear thumping or banging whenever I'm downstairs in the kitchen. I'd come up to look but find nothing."

"At least we can rule out a poltergeist, they tend to follow children... and young children at that."

"You mean like the movie? I thought that was a bunch of Hollywood bologna." She arched a brow; the hint of her earlier judgmental look still lingered.

I chuckled at her use of bologna. She definitely had that "mom tone" going on. "Pretty much, though poltergeists are very real and they tend to stick to the person they're haunting."

"Well I hope you know what you're doing. I'm going to bed. Goodnight... *Onyx*." The way she said my name seemed a little sarcastic.

"Sleep tight, Mrs. Sanders." I had a habit of responding to sarcasm with some of my own, though I tried to work on my social etiquette when it came to clients. This time, I couldn't resist a little "Vincent Price" in my tone.

Midnight finally rolled around and still no peep from the equipment. I checked the levels again. Outside of a normal temperature drop, nothing. "What a bust." Most hauntings turned out to be complete bullshit like leaky pipes; but I was sure this was something. Mrs. Sanders was a rational person who only came to me out of desperation. She had a lot riding on resolving this.

I looked into the mirror to see if my necklace had changed color. Yet *another* unreliable tool. As awesome as Aunt Belinda's intentions were, every tool of the trade she handed down to me never seemed to work properly when I needed it to. In this case, my jade amulet. It had a tendency to go black when something paranormal was about to go down. I say tendency though what I really mean is once... only once had it done that.

I tapped it. "This thing on?" I asked with a giggle.

Speaking of black, my eyeliner looked uneven. I went back to my duffel bag to grab my makeup pouch when the sound of the EMF blasted through the bag, startling me. I was sure I had turned it off. I pulled it out and took a look at it. Not only was it on, but the needle was going crazy. Without wasting another second, I checked the temperature gauge and the motion sensor. Still nothing. I flipped off the lights and turned on the night vision camera. Not a damned thing.

Rather than deal with a screeching EMF in the dark, I turned the lights back on and walked around the room with it, trying to pick up the strongest point—which happened to be the closet. "Of course it would be the fucking closet."

I took a deep breath and flung open the door, batting the clothes around in an effort to stave off a jump scare. Even in movies, they were a ridiculous and an unnecessary tactic used as an excuse for lazy storytelling. The last thing I needed was to have them in my real life. A wispy puff of white formed in front of my face as I slowly exhaled. *Uh oh.* The insistent beeping of the temperature gauge confirmed the air had chilled.

"Okay, buddy. I don't know what you want, but you need to leave this nice lady and her daughter alone." A quick mirror check showed my necklace was still green. "Thanks, Aunt Belinda," I muttered, sarcastically.

Now it was time for the big guns. I went back to my bag to grab the kosher salt and sage. Per the instructions left to me by my aunt, I sprinkled some salt in all four corners of the room and lit the sage. Though I didn't believe in any set religion, any time I burned the sage, I made the sign of the cross with it via air symbols. Sage was a Native American tactic while the symbol of the cross represented more of a Catholic type. Whenever I had the chance, I'd combine as many relevant religions as I could in one action… *just in case.*

As I finished the last corner, the temperature went back to normal and the EMF went completely silent.

Dealing with ghosts isn't as extreme as one would think. If you come in with a plan and have some sense of what to do, most of the time you can get rid of it yourself without having to elicit the assistance of a paranormal investigator.

Just like STDs, most of them can be avoided by using preventative measures. In this case, I tell new home owners to sprinkle salt and burn sage before moving in… or at least soon after. The local real estate office has banned me from the premises for this very reason. When I first started on this little endeavor, I'd hand my card out to everyone entering or exiting the building. Printed on the front was my name and number; on the back, a supernatural check list for new home ownership. I was nine.

I'm thirty now… and the ban is still in effect.

My aunt told me to wear it like a badge of honor.

"Well, my work here is done," I said in a mock-southern accent. Still, I decided to stay the rest of the night, just in case.

When I woke up the next morning, I checked the night vision camera recording to catch any reoccurrences of our little ghost. Nada.

Mrs. Sanders knocked on the door. "How was it? Anything?"

"Yeah. You definitely had a ghost," I said.

"Really?" She looked distraught.

"I took care of it." I reached into my bag and handed her the remainder of the sage and salt. "Hold onto this. You may need to reapply the salt in the corners if you vacuum in here. If something happens again, burn the sage in each corner of the room, making the sign of the cross, starting with the southeast corner and ending with the southwest."

She looked confused as I handed her the items.

"Seriously though. I'm pretty sure I took care of your problem."

"Alright." She seemed unconvinced. "How much do I owe you?"

The way she asked made me feel guilty. I *had* taken care of her problem, but there was no way I could prove that without looking like a charlatan. I sighed. "Don't worry. You don't have to give me anything… unless you wanna pay for the sage and salt, which came out of my own pocket." I'm pretty sure her financial situation was fairly grim since she was dealing with the legal system.

"It's fine. I'll have a check for you when you're ready."

I packed my things and went downstairs. She was waiting for me by the door.

The check was for fifty dollars. If people ask, I tell them I charge by the hour and it's usually twenty-five unless it's an all-nighter— then I charge a $200 flat fee for the night plus out-of-pocket expenses. In certain cases, I'll go lower. Most of the time, I leave empty handed since most of my calls are of a domestic nature.

I looked at her just before stepping out the door. "I know you don't believe this… but you really did have a ghost and I took care of it. Good luck with your hearing."

"Thanks," she said. Her eyes looked more sad than relieved.

Chapter 2

Onyx

Taking public transportation anywhere was a feat. People had a tendency to stare. I mean come on, like wearing black in the twenty-first century was unusual. I'd even see the occasional old lady making the sign of the cross if she had to sit anywhere near me. Oh, the irony.

I arrived back to the shop just in time to hear porn blasting at full volume.

"Oh come on, Frank. It's eight o'clock in the fucking morning!" I called out.

It went dead silent. Dead being a relative term in the case of Frank. Frank "the Spank" Salvaggio was the resident ghost here at the Mystery Box... another part of my inheritance.

The TV screen near the cashier counter went statical. "Sorry 'bout that," I heard Frank say through it.

Normally, I'd open the shop at the ass-crack of noon, but I figured I'd get my day started early since I was up already.

"How'd it go?" asked Frank.

"She had a ghost for sure... but I took care of it."

"Look at you. Little badass all grown up." He chuckled.

"Yeah, whatever, Frank. Cool it with the porn today, okay?"

"Why should I? This is a porn shop."

"Yeah, but not everyone who comes in here is a seedy mobster."

I wanted the Mystery Box to be an acceptable place for people to shop at. Granted, most of the customers were guys looking to get off, but I also had couples who wanted to experiment, as well

11

as the ladies who came in for all of their bachelorette party needs. The last thing I wanted was to scare off would-be customers with hardcore pornography blasting through the flat screens.

Frank did enough scaring on his own.

Back in the seventies, Frank was a mid-level bookie for the mob; the Salvatore crime family to be exact. These days, the mob is just a whisper, but back in his day, they took over Philadelphia.

During one quiet spring morning in 1978, someone injected him with a fast-acting poison through one of the glory holes in the arcade here at the Mystery Box. The arcade was where men would come and "spank the monkey" to some reeled and video porn back in those days. Someone had the brilliant idea of making glory holes for a quick blowjob or handy-j. Interestingly enough, that's how he earned his nickname, "the spank."

Frank would come to the Mystery Box at least once a day.

He still denies using the glory holes though.

When my aunt took over, she broke down that area and used it for storage, turning the Mystery Box into a legitimate video rental establishment. Granted we still had a porn room in the back, she wasn't a complete idiot, but it allowed for a more respectable clientele to patronize the store.

When video rentals took a dive and online streaming became the norm, she turned the Mystery Box *back* into a porn store, though more of a high-scale one.

She died about two years ago and along with the store and my house, I inherited Frank, the horny ghost.

Recently, I'd been tempted to turn it into an arcana shop for your "everyday magical needs," but each time I bring it up, Frank threatens to drive out the customers.

One of the other benefits from having the store being a former video rental place— all the left over classic horror films.

I pushed "Night of the Living Dead" into the video player.

"Not this again," Frank groaned.

"You had all night to watch porn, Frank. This is my time, and I'm grumpy at having to be up before eleven AM. Besides, there's a TV in the back."

"But it's black and white and shitty."

"So. It'll be more authentic then."

"We had color TV in the seventies you know."

"Yeah, yeah."

He finally went away.

The local hoodlums made sure to leave my store alone since I had such an effective guard dog. After over thirty years of "mysterious occurrences" at the shop, it made it to the list of Philadelphia's most haunted buildings. Something which increased the customer base.

Aunt Belinda, a medium and the store's previous owner, wasn't so impressed with the status. She threatened to turn it into a palm reading business before ever having it go back to a porn establishment. Since it was our only means of income, I convinced her to do otherwise. Frank had a helping hand in that as well.

Since I opened the shop early, the foot traffic was light. In turn, I closed up before actual closing time and headed home. The nice thing about the store was that it was located only a few blocks from my house.

One might consider me lucky with everything I received from my aunt's estate. Personally, I'd rather have my aunt. Of all the things I got, however, the house was by far my favorite. It was an old, two-story Victorian with both an attic and a basement. Oddly enough, it was *not* haunted.

****

It was too early to turn in and also a Friday night, so staying home wasn't a viable option. I didn't have many friends except George, Lisbeth, and those I saw at Awakening— a Goth club in Old City.

After my shower, I tossed on some baggy pants and a bodice over my tank top. I wasn't feeling especially sexy today after my night of ghost-busting and day at the porn store, so I kept my look more "scary industrial girl," instead of my usual "steampunk goddess."

Though I didn't look my age, I felt as if I was the oldest person at Awakening. Especially since those I socialized with were all in their early twenties.

"Onyx! You finally came." Lisbeth ran over and hugged me.

"Hey. Yeah. Sorry about that. It's been a busy few weeks for me." One of the things I enjoyed most about hanging around Lisbeth, is how she always smelled like peppermint. I wasn't sure if it was just her or leftover Christmas body lotion.

"You missed *all* the drama."

"Uh oh. What happened?" I asked.

"That guy, Guy? You know the one who likes to bring underage girls to the club. Yeah, he finally got busted. The cops had this place on lockdown for the rest of the night and carded everyone. They found like a dozen kids with fake ID's... it was intense."

I chuckled a bit. "I'll bet. So is Guy in jail?"

"Yeah, he got arrested... not sure what happened after though."

"Good riddance, that fucker was a total perv."

"Solve any good mysteries, Scooby?" Lisbeth asked with a giggle.

"Yup. Rousted a ghost from this lady's house just last night."

"I still think you're just a clever con artist... convincing people they have ghosts and shit. Ghosts are about as real as those vampire assholes in the back booths."

I looked up to the "vampires" she was referring to and lo and behold, the back booths were once again filled with douchebags. At least they weren't real vampires.

As I watched the crowd of poseurs drinking their goblets of "blood," one of them stood out among the others. This guy was way too good looking for that particular group. Seeing anyone, good looking or bad, pretending to be a vampire, had left me jaded over the years. Even the sort-of hot guys always ended up ugly. Don't get me wrong, I appreciate good theatrical makeup and role playing any day of the week, but these guys were just sad.

The good looking guy locked eyes with me for a moment. "Shit."

"What?" Lisbeth asked.

"Fucking eye contact. I need to *not* gawk at people here. Everyone just wants to make conversation and it eventually leads to awkward rejection. I'm a total shit-head magnet."

She looked over to the man I was referring to. "He's not that bad, actually."

He definitely had a seductive quality in the way he moved and looked at me. *Maybe I misjudged the vampire crowd altogether…* my thoughts seemed to drift into a daze. I couldn't take my eyes off this gorgeous man. As he approached, I caught his scent which caused me to snap out of it. "Oh god." I coughed a bit and held my hand over my face.

"What is it?" Lisbeth asked.

"That smell. Oh my God. I'm going to puke." *Damn it, this one actually* is *a vampire.*

He furrowed his brows as he stepped closer.

"Bro… just… just go away," I said, my sounds muffled through my hand.

"Excuse me?"

It dawned on me as to why I was so entranced with him before I caught his scent; he was using his abilities on me. My aunt told me it was a cross between being stoned out of your mind and watching a really great movie. Though I'd never experienced a vampire in person, I was educated on what to expect… and smell. She wasn't kidding.

"You *actually* smell like garbage," I found myself saying without thinking.

Not that Lisbeth believed any of my stories, I was always careful when making factual statements about the supernatural world. There were repercussions for those who blabbed. My aunt never got into the details of what they were, exactly, or who made the rules; she just said they were there and there for good reason.

The man, or rather, the vampire, scowled at me. "That's not a polite thing to say to someone."

"Well that's not a polite odor. Jesus fucking Christ."

"I don't smell anything," Lisbeth said.

That's because you're not me.

"Ah. I see what's happening here. *You're one of those.*"

There isn't exactly a name for what I am, and if there were, my aunt never told me. She *did* tell me, however, there would be entities or creatures who would know what I am and of my abilities. And that they knew to stay away... most of the time.

The vampire stood there, smirking. These days, supernatural creatures who had some semblance of control, made sure to keep the violence to a minimum. If this guy was here, he probably obeyed the same rules I did. Though I didn't care how cute or tame he was; he was ultimately a blood sucking villain who smelled like rotting garbage.

"I will rob a blood bank for you if you just please go away before I puke."

He shook his head and finally walked away.

"What was that about?"

"He just needed a shower."

Lisbeth sniffed her armpits. "I'm telling you, I don't smell anything. You're crazy. He's cute though. Maybe if I catch him, I'll have a shot."

"Please don't. Do you want to get sucked into the douchebag club, *literally?*"

"You're right. I have a reputation to maintain." She flipped her long, black hair over her shoulder.

I looked to the vampire crowd once more. *Little do they know...*

Any prospect of getting laid was quashed by Mr. Garbage, and now I just wanted to get home and crawl into bed. The lack of sleep from the night before, as well as having to deal with Frank all day, had worn me out.

16

Chapter 3

Elliot

I could hear my phone ringing from the shower. Half soaped up, I rushed out to answer it.

"This is Detective Stevens."

"We have a potential homicide in Overbook. I'll text you the address." It was Nicki. For once, she was up before me.

I quickly finished my shower and threw on my grey suit. Though my morning ritual was a bit more involved, today I had to leave the house looking a bit more scruffy than usual.

"Who's our vic?" I asked Nicki just as I arrived at the scene.

"ID says Evelyn Sanders. Her ex-husband was dropping off their daughter when he found her at the bottom of the stairs."

I squatted down and examined the body.

"My guess is she tripped and fell down the stairs," Nicki added.

I looked up at the Medical Examiner. "What do you think, Roger?"

"Oh you know me, I think all kinds of things. However a simple trip and fall is unlikely. Based on the temp, she died around midnight and the trajectory is a bit too far to be a tumble down the stairs." He gave me a coy smile.

Sometimes I couldn't tell if he was flirting with me or just being funny.

"I'll let you know more when I get her on the table," he said.

"Where's the ex?" I asked, standing back up.

"In the kitchen with his daughter," Nicki said.

I followed Nicki to the kitchen and saw Mr. Sanders comforting his sobbing daughter.

"Mr. Sanders?" I asked.

He nodded.

"I'm Detective Stevens… this is Detective Alcott. First, let me share my condolences on your loss. I know this isn't an easy scene to walk into."

"Thank you," he said.

"I just have a few questions… standard. When did you see your wife last?"

"Wednesday evening, when I picked up Lily."

"Was this prearranged?"

"Yes. Evelyn and I are… were… on a verbal agreement for shared custody. We were in the process of having a formal agreement drawn up."

"I see… and where were you last night? Again, it's just a formality." People tend to get defensive and nervous when I question their whereabouts. If I keep it simple with a heads up and they are still nervous, they tend to have something to hide.

"I understand. I was at home with my fiancée and Lily," he said.

"If it's alright, I'd like to confirm with your fiancée."

"Of course."

I looked at Lily and gave a half-smile.

She looked up at me, then her father, before looking down. It was never an easy process to gauge a child's mood or behavior. They seemed to be confused during traumatic events. This look, on the other hand, raised some questions.

"Do you have anything to add, Lily?" I asked her. "Any questionable people hanging around your mother lately?"

"Tell her, Daddy," she said to her father.

He took a deep breath.

"Tell us what?" I asked.

"It's ridiculous. Lily is convinced this house is haunted. It's why I picked her up on Wednesday. She refuses to sleep in her bedroom. At first, we both wrote it off… but then Lily was having panic attacks. I told Evelyn she had to take care of it or I'd bring it up at the custody hearing."

Bingo.

"Alright. If you don't mind waiting here for just a few more minutes." I turned to Nicki and whispered. "Let's check the bedroom. Might want to bring someone from CSU, just in case... these never turn out good."

She nodded.

I left the kitchen and did a quick once over of the room before I let CSU do a thorough investigation. "So much pink," I muttered. I walked back to Nicki. "Pull her phone records. Let's see if there was a boyfriend in the picture."

Nicki pulled out her phone and walked outside while I headed back to the kitchen.

"Anything unusual?" I asked one of the techs.

"Nope."

"Alright. Can you go help upstairs?"

"Right away, detective."

Nicki came back in. "They'll have something for us as soon as we get back."

Something on the counter caught my attention. I picked it up. "What's this?"

Nicki looked at it for a moment before taking it and smelling it. "Sage." She picked up the box of kosher salt next to it. "Huh."

"What?"

"Nothing. Just interesting that she would have sage and kosher salt... together."

"Why is that interesting?" I asked.

She cleared her throat. "Occult stuff."

"Ah yes, your post before this one." I chuckled a bit. Something else on the counter caught my eye: a black business card underneath where the box had been. "*Onyx Investigations.* This ever come up at all during your old position?" I handed the card to Nicki.

"Nope. Can't say I've heard of it. Seems like Mrs. Sanders was taking this ghost business seriously, though."

CSU finally came back down.

"Anything?" I asked.

"Aside from salt sprinkled around the corners of the room... nothing out of the ordinary. No fluids, nothing."

"Something was traumatizing this girl while she was here. Perhaps Mrs. Sanders did in fact have a boyfriend she didn't tell anyone about."

"Maybe... wouldn't be the first time," Nicki said.

I turned to Mr. Sanders. "Mind if I use your bathroom?"

He shook his head. "Go right ahead."

CSU would have gone through the medicine cabinets already, but I had a habit of taking a look for myself. Their job was to document the facts and my job was to see the bigger picture.

I closed the medicine cabinet only to see the shadow of something behind the shower curtain through the mirror. I quickly turned around and pushed it open; nothing. Oddly enough, the room felt colder than usual. When I pulled the curtain back and checked the mirror again, the shadow was gone. It took a lot to make me feel uneasy. All I knew was, I had to get out of this bathroom.

"Everything okay?" Nicki asked as I stepped out.

"Yeah, fine. Let's go check out this 'Onyx Investigations.'"

Chapter 4

Onyx

"You know, Frank, you were around the Goth scene just as it was starting out. I would have killed to have been alive then."

"Wasn't my thing," Frank said.

Saturday was more of a busier day because of the bridal showers and bachelorette parties. Though I had a tendency to laugh at some of the ridiculous novelty items I sold at the Mystery Box, it didn't stop me from making use of some of the functional ones like the penis cake pan. It even allowed me to be creative when it came to baking; figuring out all the ways I could turn it into a legit image with the expert use of frosting.

I pulled out my compact and reapplied my burgundy lipstick. With my makeup, I preferred reddish tones. They had a tendency to make my hazel eyes pop, though you could say my eyes were more of a gold color than anything. If I stared at people for too long, they usually freaked out because of it. Then again, that could have been for a number of reasons.

"Margaret Mitchell?"

I looked up to see a man standing just inside the front entrance. He was dressed in a grey suit and sported a cool demeanor. Actually, he was quite hot… for a normie. Though hearing my name tended to put me in a foul mood. "Who's askin'?"

He held up his badge as he walked over to me. "Detective Elliot Stevens."

"My name is Onyx."

"Well that's not the name on the deed to this building. It says here" —he lifted his phone— "it's under the name Margaret Vivien Leigh M—"

"Stop. Please. Don't say that name. I've killed people for less."

"Really? Because I'm investigating a murder."

Poor choice of words.

"So are you… her… or not?"

"Yeah, I am. But sorry, I don't know of anyone who was murdered… unless something happened at the club after I left?"

He pulled out a notepad. "What club?"

My eyes went wide. "Um, Awakening. Did something happen?" The presence of that vampire had me worried. Maybe he or someone else broke the rules.

"And how long were you at this club for?"

"I left around 12:30, why?"

"May I ask why a Mrs. Evelyn Sanders had your business card?"

I froze for a moment. "Is Mrs. Sanders alright?"

"If you would answer me, please."

"Um… she had a bit of a paranormal problem. Something was harassing her daughter. She hired me to look into it." I reached into my drawer, pulling out the undeposited check and staring at it for a moment before handing it to the detective. "I guess it would be wrong for me to deposit it now. Not that I was going to anyway."

He looked up at me. "Why not?"

"I dunno. She's a single mom dealing with a custody battle and a scared child. I kind of felt bad about taking it in the first place."

He handed the check back to me. "When did you see Mrs. Sanders last?"

"Friday morning. I stayed over to help take care of her ghost problem."

"And did you find any ghosts?" he asked, patronizingly I might add.

"Yes, I did actually."

"So tell me… how does one find ghosts?"

"Are you asking me to make fun of me or do you really want to know?" I asked.

"I'm just curious as to why she had sage and kosher salt readily available."

"I gave it to her… in case it came back."

"We found salt in the corners of her daughter's room. I take it that was your doing?"

"Yes."

"What other 'things' do you use?"

"If you really want to know, I'll show you." I got up and headed toward the back room.

"I don't like cops," I heard Frank say through the black and white TV.

"Not now, Frank. The lady I was helping the other night, died."

"How?"

"I'm not sure. Ghosts can't kill people… outside from annoying them to death."

"Reel that sass back in, ya smarmy broad."

"Or what?" I asked.

There was no response.

"Thought so."

I came back out with my duffel bag only to find a woman standing next to the detective. As I got closer, a strong odor emanated from her. I held my hand to my mouth and nose as I set the bag down.

"What?" Detective Stevens asked.

I glared at the woman beside him. "Nothing."

He followed my gaze. "This is Detective Nicki Alcott. She's investigating Mrs. Sanders' homicide with me."

He sorted through the duffel bag. "So what is this stuff— could you stop doing that please?" he asked, looking back up at me.

I hesitantly removed my hand and swallowed, trying to hold my breath.

Detective Alcott scowled at me.

Detective Stevens smelled the air a bit. "Does something smell bad?"

I nodded. "Like wet dog." Which meant the woman beside him was a werewolf. *Odd.* I never thought supernatural creatures would ever be a part of law enforcement.

She smelled the air around her. "I smell nothing except old cigarettes and lubricant," she said as she glanced further into the shop.

At least she didn't know what I was, unlike the vampire from last night.

I picked up a can of air freshener and sprayed the air. It would be a temporary bandage at least until she left.

She continued to scowl at me. The last thing I wanted to do was clue her into my knowing what she was.

I looked into the bag. "Anyway... this is an EMF, this is a camera" —I gave him a 'duh' look— "and this gauges the temperature in the room. There are a few other things in there... motion detector, a flood light... the usual."

"'The usual,'" he mimicked with a chuckle.

"So Thursday night, the temperature dropped and the EMF went nuts around midnight, so I burned some sage and sprinkled a little salt. It usually does the trick. Though ghosts are more annoying than violent," I said a little louder while looking upward.

"No holy water or religious icons?" Detective Alcott asked.

What did she know of it? "No. I was trying to roust a spirit, not exercise a demon."

"I see. And *you're* the professional."

"You're damn right I am." I put everything back in the bag and set it on the ground behind the register.

"Detective Alcott was with a special division prior to this job. She dealt with things of this nature so she knows a thing or two."

"Does she?" I gave her a patronizing stare. The smell was coming back which affected my ability to sass her properly. "Ugh. Seriously, lady. Take a bath... wait... that might make it worse. Forget I said anything."

She stepped forward and slammed her hands on the counter, clearly getting ready to say something unkind, when Detective Stevens put his arm in front of her, signaling her to stand down. She shook her head, grumbling, then stormed out.

"You shouldn't antagonize cops like that," Detective Stevens said.

I looked up at him. It was easier to study his face now that he was closer. His eyes were a steel grey color which matched his suit. *Sexy.* And with the "dog" gone, I could catch his scent as well. "You smell like cotton candy and honey."

Along with the bad, there were good scents as well. They usually came from good people and certain supernatural creatures. Everyone had a defining scent. Those in the same grouping, like vampires, would smell the same with slight variations. Good people smells always varied no matter what. I never understood why or how and Aunt Belinda never explained it to me.

He cleared his throat and stepped back. "Perhaps it's my cologne."

"What is it?"

"It's called 'Angel.'"

I lifted myself and leaned forward to catch another scent. It was rare that I smelled something so good and delicious.

"Stop that," he said as he jerked back some. "It's very weird."

I smirked a bit and went back to my position behind the counter. It was interesting that he wasn't immediately repelled by the way I looked. For many men, the Goth girl theme was a turn off; especially to normies, as I like to call them.

He did a quick glance around. "So you run this place?"

"Yes. My aunt left it to me when she died."

"So this is your day job? And at night you're a ghost-buster."

"A girl needs to put food on the table," I said with a smile.

"And you live alone?"

How presumptuous. "That I do. Just me."

"What about co-workers or employees?"

I chuckled a bit. "Just me and Frank, the dead mobster who haunts this place."

The TV on the counter flipped on to loud static, to which I started laughing.

It startled Detective Stevens; he didn't find it funny. "It would be unwise to upset two cops in one day."

I lifted my hands. "I swear, it wasn't me." I reached over and manually turned off the TV. "Stop it, Frank! You're going to get me arrested."

Speaking about the supernatural world and providing actual proof was a big no-no. Getting rid of spirits from your every-day home was a bit of a grey area. See, people know about ghosts, but they don't *know* there are ghosts. It was another one of the rules.

It's easier to walk the "grey" line because of how disbelieving people are. No matter how much proof one could produce, the human brain didn't seem capable of accepting the truth of the paranormal. In the case of people being haunted, they are either viewed as disturbed or wanting attention. Either way, I didn't want to push it.

"So you really believe this stuff?"

"It's my life," I said. "That and porn." I gestured my hand the same way a model would on a game show.

He stepped forward again and handed me his card. "If you think of anything else, give me a call."

My mind went back to Mrs. Sanders again. If a spirit *was* involved, her case would end up a cold one or worse, someone innocent would go down for the crime. "I don't think anyone killed her."

"No?"

"At least no one living."

He furrowed his brows at me. "If there were tons of angry ghosts roaming the world, don't you think more people would end up dying mysterious deaths? In my line of work, there is always a bad guy."

He was right. There usually is a bad guy. Most violent supernatural creatures existed in some physical form or another. I worried this was something else entirely. I talked a great game, but I was still a novice learning the ropes.

"I hope you get him... whoever it is."

"Me too." He looked at me a moment before leaving.

"Thank you, Jesus. He's gone."

"Shut up, Frank. He's a nice guy."

"No cops are nice. They are always working some angle," Frank said.

Maybe so.

Elliot

"So what happened after I left?" Nicki asked.

"I just had a few more questions." I chuckled. "So what's with the dog thing? I didn't know you owned a dog."

"I don't." She looked forward, seemingly distracted.

"You okay?"

"Yeah. Let's get back... we have some things to go over."

"That girl was a little strange, don't you think?" I asked as I pulled away from the Mystery Box.

"Here's hoping we don't have to come back here unless it's to arrest her."

I laughed again. "For what?"

"Being rude."

"She wasn't that bad." *She really wasn't.* I had to admit, the act of her "smelling" me, whatever that was about, really turned me on.

"I know her type. They pretend to be into the occult and get themselves involved in all sorts of shenanigans. Stupid teenagers."

I looked at my phone again. "Says here she's thirty."

"Let me see that." She grabbed my phone and looked for herself. "Whatever. It must be all that makeup."

"Must be."

She looked at me again, almost like she were evaluating every inch of me. Sometimes she was obvious about it, sometimes she wasn't, but I would occasionally catch her staring at me. Heck, even some of her comments were a little suggestive at times. "You're a boy scout. There's no need for you to get mixed up in that world."

"As opposed to you?"

She flashed a grin and locked her gaze with mine with those big brown eyes of hers. If she wasn't my partner, she'd be someone I'd ask out on a date... especially with all her persistence.

****

Back at the station, we went over the phone records and bank transactions of Mrs. Sanders.

"Nothing out of the ordinary, save for a couple of calls to Ms. Mitchell which confirms her story," I said.

"This is going to be a cold one... I know it." Nicki groaned as she sat back at her desk.

"We should go see the M.E. tomorrow."

"You know I think he has a crush on you." She arched a brow.

He wouldn't be the only one, I thought as I looked at her. "Too bad. I don't date co-workers," I said as I turned back to my computer. "Also, I'm straight."

Onyx's mention of a ghost got me wondering. I did a quick search of "Mystery Box" and "dead mobsters" with the name "Frank."

Something came up in the archived database for cold case files. The department finally had the good sense to digitize all the old data. It showed Frank Salvaggio, a member of the Salvatore crime family, was murdered on April 1st 1978 at a location known as the Mystery Box, 25 Parson Ave. He was injected with an aconite solution via syringe which was found at the scene.

Not that this information gave any truth to the situation. Onyx could just be a delusional girl or someone with a penchant for telling lies. *Don't be so quick to judge.* Maybe another interview was warranted.

"Hey. Wanna get something to eat?"

I looked up and smiled at another one of Nicki's attempts to socialize outside the office. "I am good, I think. Rain check?"

"Yeah, sure."

One of these days I'd have to say yes, at least on a professional level, lest I come out looking like a jerk.

I did another run on Onyx's file. "A sealed record... bad girl," I muttered to myself. Though I couldn't imagine she *wouldn't* admit to whatever it was. More recently, she had been picked up for breaking and entering, trespassing, and an assault at Awakening—though all the charges ended up being dropped... even for the assault.

I laughed when I read the details of the assault report. One of the club goers was reportedly harassing girls and lifting skirts. When the bouncer tried to deal with it, he was attacked and knocked out. Ms. Mitchell took it upon herself to step in.

"Bad girl, indeed," I said again.

Chapter 5

Onyx

"I really need to hire someone. Today has been a nightmare. How many people are getting married in this city for fuck's sake?"

"Are you saying no to free money?" Frank asked.

"No... it's not that. I just feel responsible for Mrs. Sanders. I must be off my game. What the hell did I miss? Aunt Belinda never told me ghosts could be so violent... annoying... but not violent."

"If it even was a ghost. You can just go there tomorrow. Back in my day, businesses were closed on Sundays," he said.

"Yeah well back in your day, women had more hair on their crotch than they did on their head." I leaned against the counter and stared at the front door just in time to see a surprise visitor. "George!" I called out.

"What is it with us missing each other at the club? You don't show up two weeks in a row... then you finally go on the weekend I'm out of town." He walked over and leaned on the other side of the counter, facing me. "And how is my little queen of the night?"

"Shitty."

He gave me an over-the-top frowny face. "Did one of those douche-pires spike your drink?"

"No. One of my clients died."

"Yikes. Shitty indeed."

"Her house was haunted. I thought I fixed it and boom, cops found her dead this morning. They even came to the shop to question me. By the way, you missed the hottest cop ever."

"I can't believe you still do all that paranormal stuff... and that people actually pay you. I would think you were a cruel con artist if you didn't actually believe in it."

"Don't be rude... or I won't tell you your eyeliner is smudged."

He gasped and grabbed my compact from the counter top. "Bitch," he said as he ran his finger under his eye. "No matter what I do, I just can't seem to perfect the smokey-eye."

"In time, my friend, in time."

"So Lisbeth tells me you drove off one of the few legitimately hot guys at the club last night."

I'm sure he was referring to the real vampire. "He hung out with the vamp wanna-be's, you know those guys can never be hot."

"If it's the same guy I saw last weekend... yes they can."

"He's been there more than once?" Funny, I didn't notice him the last time I was at Awakening.

"Yup. The first night you didn't show up, in fact."

Odd.

"Anyway, I'm here for supplies. I've got a new beau."

"Ooh, dish," I said with a coy smile.

"He's a lawyer. Total normie. I caught him gawking at me while I was getting coffee at the Bean."

"So you're converting people now?"

"Not really. He did one of those cold-war super spy moves by discreetly handing me his business card before casually walking out the door. Turns out, he's totally into bondage and you know me... I can't refuse a top."

"Alright then, shop away." He stepped in the back before I called out to him. "And stay away from the leather! That shit is expensive."

I had a habit of hooking my friends up with free porn and toys. Condoms were also a given. Though it's eighteen and older, and even says so on the front door, I'd get teenagers wandering in on occasion. Before I'd kick them out, I'd hand them a free condom and tell them to stay safe. I consider it my civic duty regardless of how prudish our country is as a whole.

"Fuzzy cuffs? Really?"

George grinned sheepishly. "What? You know metal leaves marks."

He ended up leaving with a pair of cuffs, some lube, and a butt plug.

It was an arrangement of sorts with us. I gave him expensive toys, he hooked me up with expensive clothes from the alternative clothing store he worked at across town. The only difference being, I was the owner of this establishment—he was not the owner of his. As long as we both stayed away from the really pricey stuff, no one seemed to pay it any mind. The shop he worked at had these full-sized pair of black angel wings I would eventually have to save up for since they were nearly $500. The quality on them was amazing.

"How is our little fairy this evening?"

"Frank, you can't say shit like that these days."

"Why not?" he asked.

"Maybe if you turned on the news instead of watching porn all day, you'll see times have changed."

"Nah. I don't like the news. Too violent."

I just shook my head.

****

At nine, I closed up shop, taking my duffel bag with me to Mrs. Sanders' house. There wasn't much I could do for Mrs. Sanders, but I'd be damned if I let someone else fall prey to a violent entity.

With any luck, the salt and sage would still be there though if it didn't work last time, what's to say it would help me now?

The police seal on the front door proved to be an issue, however.

I snuck around back to check the doors and windows. "Rats." They were all locked. It made sense for the first floor to be on lockdown, but that didn't mean the second floor was.

As I climbed up the lattice, I heard a voice echo from below me.

"What are you doing?"

I tried to look at the person over my shoulder, but only lost my grip. "Fuck!"

Half expecting to break my ass with a fall, I fell into the arms of my new sexy detective friend, which only caused him to stumble and fall himself. I quickly got up and helped him.

"I should arrest you for trespassing."

"Wouldn't be the first time," I said, while brushing grass off my mini skirt.

"I know. I've seen your file." He reached down and picked up his flashlight before clicking it off. "What are you doing here? This is an active crime scene."

"I don't want anyone else getting hurt."

"What makes you think someone else will get hurt?"

"I'm beginning to think I didn't do my job correctly and now there's some angry spirit roaming around this house."

"And what did you plan on doing tonight?" he asked.

The truth was, I didn't know. It dawned on me I should have checked my aunt's journals before heading here. "What do *you* plan on doing when the next owner turns up dead?"

"That's it." He pulled out his handcuffs. "Turn around."

"What?"

"You're under arrest. Let's go."

"You know if you wanted to get me in handcuffs so badly, I have tons at the store."

He pushed me against the side of the house, it wasn't rough but it was definitely forceful. "I think there's more to this than you're letting on, and I do not like being lied to." He slapped on the cuffs and escorted me to his car.

"Wait, my bag. That stuff is really expensive," I said.

He put me in the back seat and grabbed my bag before heading back to the car.

As I looked at him, something in the upstairs window caught my eye.

He followed my gaze and saw it too. "Stay right here," he said, pulling out his gun.

"Where am I gonna go? Hey, wait! You can't go in there alone. A gun isn't gonna do shit!"

"Just don't move." He continued toward the house.

"Detective Stevens! Seriously, don't go in there… at least uncuff me. I can help."

Maybe the rational part of his brain took over… or I guess in this case, the irrational part. He walked back over to the car and let me out before uncuffing me. "If you run, we're going to have a problem."

"I swear. I'm not going anywhere." I picked up my bag and followed him into the house.

"Just stay behind me and don't touch anything."

"I need the salt and sage… is it still here?"

He looked back at me.

"Seriously."

He sighed. "Yes. It's in the kitchen. I can't believe I'm going along with this. You have no idea how much trouble I can get in for having you in here."

I branched off and grabbed the sage and salt before rejoining him and following him up the stairs.

With each step, I felt the temperature drop. I quickly pulled out the temp gauge from my bag and flipped it on. It immediately started beeping.

"What's that?" he asked.

"The temp thingie I showed you earlier."

"'Thingie?'"

"What? Keep moving," I said.

"So you're in charge now?"

I sighed.

He looked forward again and slowly resumed climbing the stairs.

Since the EMF was handy in this case, I pulled it out as well.

He quickly glanced back at the sound.

"EMF," I said, giving him a quick glance. "We need to check out the kid's room."

"No. I'm going to check everything on the way there and you're going to stay behind me."

"I'm telling you, it's not some guy—it's a ghost."

"Quiet," he snapped in a hushed tone.

I turned down the sound for the EMF as we continued up the stairs. The first door was the door to Mrs. Sanders' room. He stepped in and made a motion for me to stay against the wall just inside while he checked the closet and the bathroom.

When he saw everything was in the clear, he continued in the hall, checking each door. One was to a small hall closet and the other was to a bathroom, both of which were empty.

Finally, we made it to the last door which was the little girl's room.

The EMF needle began spiking as I stepped inside. "See, I told you."

"There's no one here."

"Nope. Something is here...." I headed toward the closet again. This time, the EMF dropped. Though when I got to the bed, it spiked again. "Reach in my bag and pull out the sage and my lighter."

"You're kidding right?"

"Do it."

He sighed and dug through my bag. The first thing he pulled out was my black lace bra.

"Oh so that's where it went," I said as I saw it.

He groaned and shoved it back in the bag before finally pulling out my lighter and sage.

"Okay light it up then blow out the flame."

Again, he was hesitant.

"Seriously, bro."

He lit it and handed it to me.

"I need you to grab the salt and sprinkle it in the corners of the room."

"I'm sorry, this is becoming ridiculous—"

His words were cut by a sudden rush of ice cold air blowing around us, knocking the EMF out of my hand. I snatched the box of salt from Detective Stevens' hand and quickly made a salt circle around us. He lifted his flashlight and we could see a dark shadow swirling around the room.

"What's going on?"

"Don't move and don't step out of the circle"

His breathing increased as he brought his gun to the ready.

"That's not going to help any. Trust me. Just stay inside this circle." I lifted the sage and motioned the signed of the cross in each cardinal direction.

"Funny, you don't strike me as the religious type."

"I'm not. This is just the way I learned to do it." Once I finished, the shadow seemed to dissipate and the room came back to its normal temperature. "We should go before it comes back." I stepped outside the circle and grabbed my EMF before packing it up with the rest of the items.

It took him a second to get his bearings on the situation and follow me out the front door. "I don't understand. What just happened back there?"

"That, my friend, is a very unhappy ghost. I'm going to have to research this a bit more and come back."

"You can't come back here. Like I said—"

"Yeah, yeah, active crime scene. Whatever, boy scout. Your rules don't apply to me."

The last sentence seemed to set him off. "That's it. Turn around."

"Oh come on, again?"

"Yup." He cuffed me once more. "Let's go."

He said nothing to me on the way to the station though he occasionally looked back at me with those sexy, grey eyes of his. I could have also pointed out the fact he hadn't read me my rights even though I highly doubted anything would come of this.

We arrived at the station and he escorted me out of the car.

"My bag?" I asked, cocking a brow at him.

He shot me a look before grabbing it and putting his other hand around my arm.

"What's this?" asked an approaching officer. He was dressed in a suit not unlike the one Detective Stevens wore, though he was much taller and tanner. Interestingly enough, he looked more Native American than anything.

"She was caught trespassing at the Sanders' crime scene."

As the man approached, I caught a pungent whiff of something... like burning wood. "Whoa." I coughed as I tried to bend my shoulder to my face.

"Apparently, she also has a keen sense of smell," Detective Stevens continued.

"Is that so?" the man asked.

"Next thing, she's going to tell you that you smell like a wet dog."

The man chuckled.

"Actually, he smells like burning wood." It wasn't bad, it was just overpowering.

The man stopped laughing and his face turned serious. "I see. So you're booking her?"

Detective Stevens glanced over to me. "I'm not sure yet."

"Why don't you bring her to my office... and I can lecture this young girl on the consequences of breaking the law."

"She isn't exactly a young girl," Detective Stevens retorted.

"Ouch. Rude much?" I snapped.

The man laughed again as Detective Stevens escorted me into the man's office. Whoever he was, he was clearly in charge.

"Would you give us a moment?" he asked Detective Stevens. "And you can remove the cuffs."

He complied with the man's request though he was clearly not happy about it.

Once the door closed, the man spoke as he sat at his desk. "I'm Sergeant Longbear. And you must be" —he pulled up something on his computer— "Margaret Mitchell?"

"Ugh, don't remind me."

"Is that like the writer of 'Gone With the Wind'?"

"Yeah."

He chuckled again. "Margaret Vivien Leigh Mitchell. Your parents must have been great fans."

"Just my mom, and yeah, she was. Please, call me Onyx instead."

He sat back in his chair and looked at me for a moment. "Actually, I think I should call you Qaletaqa."

"What?" I asked with a nervous laugh.

"At least that's the closest thing I can compare it to."

"Is that some tribal word for Onyx or something?" I asked.

"No. In a loose translation, it means guardian."

"I'm sorry, I don't understand." I narrowed my eyes at him.

He looked confused for a moment. "Do you even know what you are?"

How forward. "Do *you* know what you are?"

He laughed. "Of course. In common language, I'm called a wendigo."

My eyes widened and I glanced over my shoulder out the office window for a second. "Are you even allowed to tell me that?"

"I see you know the rules… but you don't know what you are. Interesting."

"I'm sorry. I'm a little lost."

He looked at my necklace. "Your necklace is changing colors."

I lifted the pendant; it was indeed black. For once, it was working. "Wait so you know what I am? I mean, I know what I can do… I was just never told a name, I guess. My aunt was a medium and my mother… well, she was a religious nut."

"It says here your mother died when you were nine?"

I nodded. "My aunt pretty much raised me from then on."

"And what of your father?"

I shrugged. "He skipped out when I was a baby—wait, why are you asking me all this? I thought wendigos were dangerous?"

"The ancient stories of brutality are true, but like many other creatures, we've adapted."

"So you aren't going to eat me?" I asked with a smirk.

"I see you know your lore."

"Some, not all. I'm still pretty new at this." It dawned on me that perhaps I shouldn't mention how inexperienced I was, though he came off as trustworthy.

"Ah yes, the paranormal *investigations*. And no, I will not eat you." He smiled.

"So how do you know what I am?"

"I'm aware there are many creatures in this city. Though you... you were a myth. My ancestors recanted tales of the Qaletaqa from a distant land who would seek out and slaughter those of my kind... and others. More notably, they had a distinct sense of smell which could locate the evil in one's soul."

"That doesn't sound like guardian-like behavior."

"Since the rules and laws were put into place many years ago, it has been relatively tame. In fact, those of us who obey the rules rely on the guardian to weed out those who do not."

"So basically I'm like a cop to the supernatural world. Oh sweet irony... and here I am, sitting in a police station, about to get charged for doing my job."

"I wouldn't worry about that. If Detective Stevens has brought you in, it's because you annoyed him or did something truly heinous. I can't imagine you did the latter."

"So you know his partner is a werewolf, right?"

He narrowed his eyes a moment. "I had my suspicions. I don't have ways of spotting others... that's your job. Though you must be careful. You may find yourself in trouble somewhere else and you may actually be arrested. It's better to try and do your work in accordance with the rules and laws of the human world."

"To be honest... I'm stuck. I've never heard of a ghost directly harming people. Whatever is haunting Mrs. Sanders' house needs to be dealt with. Sage and salt seem to only work temporarily. On top of which, I can't really do much without telling Detective Stevens what's really going on… and we both know that's not possible. You should know, he's seen the ghost."

"And how did he react?"

"Disbelieving, like all normies."

"'Normies'?" Sergeant Longbear smiled.

"Yeah. That's what I call guys like him." I looked over my shoulder through the office window and smiled at Detective Stevens. "Anyway. He arrested me because I told him I have to go back tomorrow night to try and get rid of whatever the hell it is."

"I'd advise you to wait a few days. I believe Mr. Sanders is having the house packed up and the real estate agency is about to put it on the market—"

"Then I absolutely cannot wait. If someone buys that house and there's a murder-happy entity roaming around—"

He held up his hand. "I know. That's why I will have Detective Stevens escort you Tuesday night, once everything calms down. It should give you more than enough time to figure out what you're up against."

"Thanks, I guess."

"Now, you're free to go. I'll have Detective Stevens drive you back home as I am leaving for the night and cannot myself." He stood up and led me over to the detective's desk.

Chapter 6

Elliot

I looked up as Sergeant Longbear approached with Onyx.

"She's free to go and I am leaving for the evening. Goodnight." He walked away before I could protest.

I looked at Onyx. "So what did you both talk about?"

She gave me a devious smile. "I think that's something you're going to have to talk to *him* about. I was told you'd be giving me a ride back?"

Oh great. What else was I volunteered for? "I have paperwork to do… it'll be a while."

She leaned in and lifted her eyes to me.

"You're not smelling me again, are you?"

"Maybe."

I adjusted in my seat a bit. "Let me just finish a couple of things and we'll leave shortly."

She flashed me another grin and sat back in the chair. There was something about her. I couldn't help but feel attracted. I cleared my throat and resumed typing.

She reached over and picked up the photo of my parents. "And who is this lovely couple?"

I grabbed the photo from her and set it back down. "My folks."

"Can I see your badge again?" she asked with a smile.

"Fine. I get it. We're going." I locked my computer and grabbed my blazer.

****

"So do all the cops get these fancy new cars?" she asked as I drove off.

"No. Just the detectives." I glanced over to her sitting in the passenger seat, legs outstretched. The sight of her fishnets stirred my blood. My attraction to her made me slightly uncomfortable; she wasn't the type of girl I normally went for.

Keep your eyes on the road.

"You're a little young to be a detective, aren't you?"

"I'm thirty-five." A scratching sound caused me to look back over to her. She was picking at her nail polish. "What are you doing?"

"Oh" —she looked down at her nails— "sorry, nervous habit."

"Why are you nervous? You got away with illegal trespassing tonight."

She smirked. I couldn't help but stare at her full lips. "Wait... where are you going?"

I looked forward. "Taking you back to—oh yeah, you don't live at the Mystery Box." *Well that's embarrassing. Real smooth, Elliot.* I pulled up the tablet in the car and looked up her address.

"You know I can just tell you my address," she said, grinning.

"It's fine. I have it here."

"That was fast."

"No, it was just a recent search so—"

"So you have my information readily available?" she asked, arching a brow at me.

I needed to get her home and fast.

We pulled up to her house. It was quite amazing actually. "So this is where you live?"

"Yup. Some people call it 'protected by the Historical Preservation Society,' I call it home."

I chuckled a bit. Her wit and antics only made me that much more attracted to her.

She moved to get out. "Aren't you going to walk me to my door, officer?"

"It's Detective... and do you really need me to?"

"Yikes. By the look of you, I'd have thought you were raised better than that." She got out and slammed the door.

I put my hand to my forehead. *I* was *raised better than that.* I stepped out of the car and caught up to her. "Wait. I'm sorry."

She glanced back at me and gave a devilish smile. "Would you like to come in for a drink? Perhaps something to eat?"

"I really shouldn't."

"You aren't on duty are you?"

"No, I'm done for the day."

She turned around and stepped toward me. "Then I don't see a problem, do you?"

I evaded eye contact and looked up at the house. "Is this place haunted too?"

"No, oddly enough, it's not." She glanced back at the house. "You'd think so by looking at it." She looked back at me. "Is *that* why you're so hesitant?" she asked.

I've known this girl for less than a day and already, I was breaking protocol and escorting her home. *What is it about her?* "No. Sorry. I'll come in for some tea."

"Tea?" She chuckled a bit.

"Is there a problem?"

"No. I make a wicked pot of tea... it's just not often I encounter men who like tea."

I followed her inside. Everything about the place was antique and Victorian; it even smelled like old books... something which reminded me of my Uncle's house in upstate New York.

She motioned for me to sit on the couch while she went into the kitchen.

"You haven't been told yet, but your boss approved my going back to Mrs. Sanders' house on Tuesday so long as you come with me," I heard her say from the other room.

"Is that so?"

"Yes."

"And how did you manage to convince him?"

There was no answer.

As I sat there, taking in the sight of the abundance of antique furniture, I began to wonder about what led up to her staying in a place like this and not going with something more modern.

The sound of a whistling tea kettle interrupted my thoughts, and moments later, she walked out with a tray in hand. It was quite adorable seeing a sassy Goth girl coming out with a dainty tea set.

She looked at me. "What?"

"Sorry, nothing. Antique teapot?" I asked, trying to keep my cool.

"Yes, it belonged to my grandmother... or so I was told." She set it down and began pouring. "How do you take it?"

"Plain, please... and thank you."

"Ah, there are those manners." She lifted her eyes to me. Something about the way she looked at me kept me on my toes... as if any moment, she would pounce me. It didn't help that her eyes were as golden as a black cat's and with every passing moment, I wanted her more and more.

Once again, she left the room. Next thing, I heard music. She came back out with a container.

"What's that?" I asked.

"Tea biscuits," she said with a smile.

As the music played, I started to recognize it. "Bauhaus?"

She raised her brows. "Very good. I didn't think you were the type."

"I listened to them when I was younger." A thought came to mind, I recalled being mildly attracted to a Goth girl in high school back in the nineties. I didn't realize she had left such an impression on me until this very moment. "You're a tough one to figure out."

"How do you mean?"

"Just the whole style and... tea and cookies... and... you're—" I paused.

"I'm what?"

"Sorry, nothing."

"No, tell me. I won't get mad."

"Most of the people I see who dress like you are much... younger... than you. Please don't take offense, it's just an observation."

She giggled. "So I don't dress my age... is what you're saying."

"No. I'm just not used to it. I shouldn't have said anything." I set my teacup down.

"Goth isn't a style, it's a calling." She laughed. "I don't know. I've just always dressed like this since..." —she thought for a moment; her smile faded— "since forever."

"I'm sorry if I touched on something personal."

The smile returned. "Nah. Just memories. I've always felt comfortable with the Goth community, style, and music. For some, it's a phase. For others, like me... well, I can't imagine myself wearing anything else in *my* coffin."

Her sentiments caused me to chuckle.

"Just remember my words when you see a wrinkly old woman in Goth attire. *That's* a lifer." She looked around the house before looking back to me. "So are you hungry? I can make you some real food if you'd like."

"You cook too?"

"Is that so shocking?"

I did it again. I was assuming and being offensive and I didn't know why. "No I—"

"It's okay. I know, I'm more domesticated than I let on." She leaned closer. "I'd be the perfect love slave too... if I actually wanted a relationship, that is." She backed away again. "So what about you? Married? Kids?"

"No and no. I was engaged once but it didn't work out."

"She two-time ya?"

"No. Nothing of the sort. I knew her back in high school and we just grew apart over the years."

"How sweet, puppy love in full bloom." She had a very theatrical way of speaking which caused me to laugh. "Her loss.

You're a good looking chap. I bet you can have any girl you want." She squeezed my upper arm. "Fit too."

I glanced at her hand then back to her.

She retracted. "Sorry."

"No, it's okay. Just not used to people touching me." And it was starting to turn me on.

"I'm very handsy, as they say. Oh, I should get that book. Especially since you're going ghost hunting with me." She immediately got up and left the room.

Onyx

Hotter than previously summarized, check. Strong enough to bend me over his lap and spank me, check. Smells like two angels having sex in heaven, check.

I knew I'd end up doing something stupid like try to jump his bones before I even found out his middle name.

Now where is that journal?

It was hiding in the trunk with all the other supernatural related items my aunt left me. This particular journal was dedicated to ghosts, spirits and poltergeists. At least it would make for easier conversation and without revealing the full enchilada. Though more specific and accurate, the book didn't differ from others on the subject at face value.

When I came back downstairs, he had taken off his jacket and tie and rolled up his sleeves. Seeing him in a relaxed state made me a little giddy. *Damn it.*

"Found it," I said while waving the journal a bit as I approached him. I sat right next to him; my leg brushed against his as I set the journal on the coffee table.

From the corner of my eye, I could see him looking at my legs. Interestingly enough, he did the same thing in the car. It made me regret not wearing a shorter skirt.

"So it says here spirits *can* become hostile if provoked enough or fueled by tension or stress in the surrounding environment. I guess this whole custody thing might have triggered it. What do you think?" I looked up at him. The way he looked at me instantly made me nervous. *Snap out of it, Onyx.*

He cleared his throat. "Maybe. I didn't ask Mr. Sanders any more about his personal dealings with the vic—Mrs. Sanders."

I looked at the journal again. "It also says I was right; using kosher salt and sage should rid the house of the spirit... but that didn't work." I sighed. "What am I missing?" I asked myself. I lay back against the couch and stretched out my legs. My thigh brushed against his again. He quickly looked up.

With anyone else at this point, I'd act like a total hussy and pull them down to kiss me. With this guy, I felt I needed to keep on point and act like a lady... maybe even present him with a challenge. Perhaps he was just a good boy looking to get a little dirty with the Goth girl... something which happened all-too-frequently back in high school. I didn't want to be someone's experiment—not this late in the game. If he was, indeed, someone wanting to dip a toe in unknown waters, he could take it somewhere else.

I stood up. "I guess I'll see you Tuesday, then."

He looked up at me. "Um, yes. Of course." He grabbed his jacket and tie then stood up, extending his hand. "Thank you for the tea."

I grabbed his hand and met it with a firm grip of my own. "Right-o officer... I mean detective. Sorry."

"You can call me Elliot."

"Alright then, Elliot."

He gave me a half-smile before I walked him out.

"Fuck." And that's why I spent so many nights sleeping alone: too much time in my own head analyzing the motives of men.

Chapter 7

Onyx

Before I opened the shop on Monday, I went over to Mrs. Sanders' to see which realty company was putting the house up for sale. "Evergreen Realty... great. Just great." Evergreen was the company which had me banned before I learned how to perfect my cursive. Though I didn't see any agents around, I *did* see a couple of moving guys. "Hey," I said as I approached.

One of the men stopped and eyed me. "Yeah?"

"I used to babysit for Mrs. Sanders and I have a few things I need to give her daughter...." Rather than outright ask what address they were dropping the boxes at, I waited for him to finish the sentence. I flashed an innocent grin for good measure.

"Oh um" —he scratched his head— "hey Jerry! Where's this stuff goin'?"

A man, who I assumed was Jerry, peeked his head from inside the house. "55 Terrace Ave."

"Thanks buddy," I said before skipping off. If anything, I felt I had to get rid of this ghost and tell Mrs. Sanders' little girl that I caught the bad guy who hurt her mom.

There wasn't much to do before Tuesday except stock up on supplies. I hadn't spoken to Elliot since our awkward Saturday night.

My subconscious was taking over and I looked sexier than normal with my makeup and dress.

"Who am I kidding?" I said, looking at myself. I pinned my black hair and angled my bangs to the side for a more retro look. There was no way I'd ease up on the eyeliner, but I smudged it for more of a sultry look and went nude pink for my lips instead of my normal burgundy.

On rare occasions, I'd wear my leather motorcycle jacket with my shredded tank top which allowed my black bra to peek through. In a way, I scolded myself for dressing so suggestively to go to a house where someone was killed. Again—my subconscious working overtime.

I needed to make an impression with Elliot. He wasn't my usual type which made it even odder I was making such an effort to impress... nay, seduce.

At least I knew the house would be cleared out making it that much easier to get rid of the ghost.

Elliot never gave me a set time on when to expect a call from him, yet I hadn't heard a peep and it was getting close to ten. The busses ran pretty sparse after nine PM, so if I wanted to keep from wasting time, I had to get going. The more I realized how violent this ghost turned out to be and how I was going about this all by myself, the less I wanted to do it. Aunt Belinda could only prepare me so much before she passed.

Outside of the occasional hiccup, the supernatural world remained relatively quiet. The existence of the rules helped out in that regard. Historically speaking, she didn't have much outside the occasional journal and trinket. Our family had come over just after the witch trials began, when things were starting to get really out of hand. Perhaps it's why Sergeant Longbear told me the Native American word for what I am. Any and all historical documents, if any existed, would be back in Europe. He could only tell me what he knew from just after the time my family came over. The Native American perspective would be different from the one in Europe... or wherever my family came from.

Going at this alone made me feel less sexy than my style of dress portrayed, and the echo of an empty house made me uneasy. At least the seal from the door was gone, and the moving guys left the back door unlocked. "Idiots."

I slowly walked up the stairs to the little girl's bedroom before setting my equipment up and waiting.

It was now eleven and nothing. "Come out, come out wherever you are, ghosty."

At this point, I was more annoyed with Elliot for flaking on me than scared about the ghost.

Midnight. Still nothing.

Something wasn't right. The last time it showed itself, there weren't any living presences in the house... which meant—

"Which means it's attached to an object. Shit."

I jumped up and quickly packed my stuff before running to catch the next bus. It had already passed by the time I got to the intersection. "Bloody hell."

Not only was I stuck from being able to get to Mr. Sanders' house, I was also stuck waiting for the next bus to head home... which wasn't for another hour. There was no way I'd call Elliot, he had his chance and he blew it. Worse yet, I didn't know anyone else with a car.

Of my tiny group of friends, *I* was supposed to be the responsible adult with her shit together. It didn't help that I refused to take stock in the peripherals. Hell, it took years for my friends to finally convince me to get a smartphone.

Everything in my life was handed down to me and I made the most of it. I didn't have time to work my way up the corporate ladder of life: buy a car, get engaged, save up, buy a house, or whatever normies do these days.

****

Tuesdays were 80s nights at Awakening. I decided to hoof it since the club was a lot closer to me than my house was. At least maybe there I could bum a ride off someone.

Eighties night at the club was a mixed bag. There were a fair share of normies who went for the throwback and a small percentage of Goths who went for the authenticity of their style—it was borderline hipster and I couldn't abide.

Also, dressing the way I did and going to eighties night tended to reveal my age to those I didn't want knowing in the first place. On the topic of vampires, in that regard, I guess it was the one thing I envied: their ageless and timeless appearance. I wouldn't mind being locked into my current appearance until the day I died, but I also didn't want to live forever… or drink blood. *Yuck.*

The DJ spinning was a friend of mine so I dropped my duffel bag off at the booth before heading to the bar.

The bartender set a two finger of straight whiskey in front of me. "I didn't order anything."

"I know. It's from him." He pointed across the bar, and there was Trashy: the sexy looking vampire.

"Great," I muttered, sarcastically. "I suppose if I accept this, he's going to come over here?"

The bartender spoke but "Trashy" nodded as if he'd heard me. I suppose I should have known.

"Fine, whatever." I downed the whiskey in one shot. It was top shelf at least.

Vampy: the garbage smelling clown, made his way over to me. He stopped at a short distance. "I don't want to offend you again," he called out.

Last time, the smell emanating from him was a lot stronger, even at that distance. I took a chance and stepped closer. It was still there though not as pungent.

"I see you're taking chances," he said.

"How do you smell… well" —I took another whiff, again, it was nowhere near like last time— "less gross?"

He furrowed his brows. "You don't know?"

"I mean, I know why you smell like trash—you're a vampire. A real one. Not like those doucheclowns on Friday nights.

He chuckled at the remark. "That I am. But you don't know why the scent has faded?"

I shook my head and eyed him. Maybe like Sergeant Longbear, he too knew more about what I was than I did.

"Come on. Let's talk somewhere quiet."

"Yo. I'm not going anywhere alone with you."

"If I were going to hurt you, I'd smell a lot worse—trust me."

"I don't understand," I said.

"That's what I need to explain to you" —he looked around— "but not here. Rules."

"I see. So you know the rules."

"Everyone does," he said with a smile.

"Fine. But if you try anything, I've got a cop on speed dial, and I will out your kind faster than you can say 'UV exposure'."

He laughed and held up his hands defensively. "Understood."

Again, if he didn't smell awful… and wasn't undead, he'd totally be my type.

Awakening used to be a strip club before it got shut down for prostitution. Not unlike my store, it had smaller backrooms formerly used for illicit behavior. In the case of the Goth club, they were converted into private booths for parties who splurged on bottle service. On Tuesday nights, they were unused and roped off.

He sat down opposite me in the booth. *How courteous.* "So what mystical revelation do you have for me tonight?" I asked.

"You're colorful, I like that. Tell me, have you ever heard the term Tutorea?"

"Can't say I have. Is it Spanish?"

"Not quite, it's Basque."

The last time I heard anything about the Basque was during world history class back in high school. "I see and what does this special word mean?"

"Guardian."

I raised my brows. "Huh."

"What?"

"Nothing. Just the other night, interestingly enough, a wendigo told me the same thing, except he used a different word."

"A wendigo? Really? And you lived to tell the tale?" he asked, mildly surprised.

"He's actually a Sergeant over at the police station on Third."

He full on laughed. "My my, they really have come up in the world, haven't they?"

"There's also a werewolf who works there too. She reeks of wet dog though."

He continued with his laughing fit. "I wish I could sniff out these creatures like you can. I'm a little envious of your gift."

"No. Trust me, you shouldn't be."

"I suppose now I should explain what I meant earlier. Tutorea have the ability to catch the scents of all sorts of creatures. I suppose you know that much."

"I sure do."

"Well then it's surprising you don't know those scents can fade over time," he said.

"No. I did not know that."

"Your abilities stem from generations of ancestors who hunted supernatural creatures. Once the rules were in place, you became the guardian... Tutorea."

"Yeah. Sergeant Longbear told me something to that effect." I leaned back against the cushion of the booth.

"Well many of us complied with the rules, and the Tutorea worked alongside those who obeyed in order to weed out those who would disrupt the peace. Perhaps it was the way you were designed—evolution or... I don't know. But the creatures who obey the rules and remain good, if you will, their scents fade over time. It's a sort of trust that develops."

"So basically you smell less bad because you're a good... vampire?"

"Yes. I'm pretty sure the next time we meet, you won't smell anything at all." There was a curl in his lips as he said the words.

"Then why did you smell so horrid on Friday? Did you kill someone or something?" I asked.

"My guess is it has something to do with instinct. To be on alert. Sort of like a fire alarm. Your body turns it off when it realizes there's no fire."

"So *you* can't tell other supernatural creatures?"

"No. That's why we have you. Most of the time I can't even pick up other vampires unless they exhibit certain traits or behaviors." He narrowed his eyes a moment. "It's interesting you don't know this already."

"My aunt taught me everything she knew and it wasn't much. My mother died when I was very young. Aside from a few books and journals… I've got nothing. Actually, you're the first vampire I've ever encountered.

He smiled. "I guess I should feel honored, Tutorea."

"Please. Call me Onyx."

"Onyx? Is that your real name?"

"Yes."

"I think not. May I?" He reached out his hand.

"Uh… sure?"

He rested it on mine for a moment. At first it felt clammy, but then a surge of warmth radiated from it.

I quickly retracted my hand. "What did you just do?"

"Margaret Vivien Leigh Mitchell."

My jaw dropped. "How in the fuck—"

"I can see recent events and immediate thoughts when I touch someone. It's only a glimpse unless I know what I'm looking for. It seems you don't like it when people say your name."

"Yeah, I don't. And I'd kindly ask you never to say it again or I'll beat you with your shoes."

He laughed. "Rome."

"What?"

"My name is Rome."

"I would say 'I think not' then touch your hand, but I don't think I'll be able to suck your real name out of your consciousness."

"My real name is Romoalt."

"Yikes. What the hell kind of name is that?" I asked.

"An old one."

"How old?"

"Are you trying to ask my age?" He narrowed his eyes.

"Maybe." I folded my arms across my chest.

"It's rude to ask someone their age."

"I thought that only applied to women."

"So you're sexist?" he asked with a smirk.

"Oh hell no. You are not going to go all 'social justice warrior' on me, mister."

"Do you know the Battle of Hastings?"

"I know *of* it… yeah."

"I was there."

"No shit. So you're like… a thousand years old?"

"Almost. That's where I died, so-to-speak, on the battlefield. I was born the tenth of October, 1044 AD."

"So you'll be exactly 1000 in thirty-three years?"

He looked up a moment and nodded. "I suppose so."

"But you're really" —I brushed through the history lesson in my head for a moment— "twenty two?"

He nodded.

"So I'm older than you? Fucking hell, I'm older than everyone in this club." I slumped back in my seat.

"How old are you? Oh wait, you're a woman, I can't ask that," he said with a hint of sarcasm.

"I'm thirty." I sighed.

"If it helps any, I wouldn't have guessed older than… nineteen."

"Thanks, I guess."

An awkward moment of silence passed before I spoke up again.

"So how do you know what I am? The wendigo cop called me a Qaletaqa. He pretty much said the same thing you did, except the fading scent part. He said the myth of what I am was told by his ancestors throughout the generations."

"Interesting. Outside of those who keep meticulous records or are old, like myself, not many know of what you are. The rules seemed to have scared everyone straight over the years. We don't have much need for your kind."

"So when did these rules come into play?" I asked.

"No one seems to know exactly. Each group has their own set of traditions and rules. Vampires learn from other vampires, about other vampires, et cetera. We only become aware of other creatures if they choose to reveal themselves to us.

"The only other Tutorea I've met was back in… 1550—Italy. Her name was Melena. She had the same initial reaction you did until she got to know me. It was the first time I decided to stop slaughtering humans for food. I relapsed during the American Revolution—don't ask. Anyway, she noticed the fading scent and realized I was harmless. She ended up explaining the rules as she knew them and told me about her kind."

"So what are these rules? I just have a general idea… first rule of supernatural club is don't talk about supernatural club." I leaned forward, resting my elbows on the table.

"Something like that. For the safety of our kind, we are forbidden to reveal ourselves. As the modern era approached, the rules included leaving humans alone completely; leaving us to find other, quiet ways to adapt. More recently, with the advent of medicine and blood transfusions as well as storing blood, vampires were given another way to adapt. Each group has its own rules based on needs, habits, and so on."

"So basically you were shit outta luck until blood banks?"

"More or less. Other groups were able to adapt early on. As far as I know, everyone is copacetic these days."

"So other than the obvious… how many groups do you know of?" I asked.

"I'll admit, I'm a bit spoiled since I've been around so long, but there are hundreds of different kinds of supernatural creatures. Some have fallen off the face of the earth completely; driven extinct by mankind, your kind, and the environment. Some aren't lucky enough to have a human form in some way or another, so they hide in the shadows… though they still have to abide by the rules."

"And no one knows who set up the rules? I just keep imagining some hidden government of the underworld." I giggled.

"Maybe. Rules for my kind were already in existence before I was turned, if that gives you some idea. I heard a rumor that the library of Alexandria housed many ancient scrolls which explained the rules better, as well as where they originated from."

"But it was destroyed."

"Yes." He smiled at my factoid.

"Hey man, I paid attention in history class. It's actually one of my favorite subjects."

"You remind me of her."

"Who?" I asked.

"Melena. She was quite brilliant and beautiful... and had a kind soul. She died of the plague in 1576."

"I'm sorry." I looked away for a moment.

"Don't be. She had a relatively full life... at least for the era. She had no children, not that I know of. Perhaps she was a relative of yours in some way. She once told me all the Tutorea came from the same family line."

"My aunt mentioned most of our family history was left behind when my ancestors came to the 'colonies' to take care of business. I guess the witch trials ended up being a red flag for the new world."

"I could definitely see that," he said.

"I suppose one of these days, I'll have to go to Europe and search out old records. Problem is, I have no idea where to begin."

"Perhaps the Basque region of France and Spain?"

"Maybe. Right now, I don't have the money for anything and I have no one to look over the shop if I decided to take a vacation. And Frank... ugh, he would just flip the fuck out if I left."

"Who's Frank?"

"This ghost. Anyway—"

"Wait, you're in direct communication with a ghost?" he asked, surprised.

"Yeah. He got bumped off while he was jerking off in one of the arcade booths back in the seventies. It's a long story. He's basically part of my 'inheritance.'" I held up air quotes.

"That's quite funny. I'll have to meet him."

"Trust me. You don't want to. He's not the only ghost problem I have these days."

"What do you mean?" he asked.

"I do paranormal investigation as a side job—"

He burst out laughing.

"What? Don't laugh! It's a legit operation."

"I know. I'm sorry. I just—" he continued laughing.

"Anyway! I was helping this lady out and she ended up dying because of this ghost."

He stopped laughing.

"Thank you," I said while staring daggers at him. "So now I'm determined to get rid of it permanently before it hurts anyone else. Problem is, I went there tonight and there's no sign of it. Worse yet, it could be attached to something which might have been packed up and sent to another house. The little girl it was terrorizing, the one whose mother died, could still be in danger."

"Well that's no good. I've experienced my fair share of hostile ghosts over the years. Albeit exceedingly rare, they can be cause for concern. I hope you know what you're doing."

"Yes... maybe. Kind of. I did the whole salt and sage thing... it went away. I thought I took care of it but then it killed that poor woman." I slumped again.

"If it is indeed attached to an object, you have to salt and burn said object. But I'm sure you already know that."

"Of course." I cleared my throat and straightened in my seat.

"Well then. You shouldn't have any issues. Now your only problem is finding the haunted object."

"Yes. Absolutely. In fact, I will be doing that tomorrow." The sound of last call echoed from the main room. "I suppose it's time to leave."

"I still have a few hours."

"Yeah but I need to find a way home in time to get a little shut-eye before I open the store tomorrow."

"And what store is that?"

"The Mystery Box. It's a porn store if you hadn't guessed by my earlier story."

A devious grin crept on his face.

"Yeah, no. Stop right there, *Twilight*. I don't do the vampire thing, thanks. Which reminds me, why do you hang out with those wanna-be weirdos?"

"I can blend in, plus they are entertaining. It's easier to be the sole focus of women looking to get lucky when you're surrounded by the opposite of a pussy magnet."

I laughed. "I like you. I think we can be friends... as soon as the smell goes away permanently."

"Oh, I should also tell you. If you find yourself around someone whose smell has faded, then suddenly comes back, it means they broke the rules. In my case, it could be anywhere from killing someone to revealing myself publically."

"So if you start to smell like trash again, I have to stake you? What am I? Buffy now?"

"Not exactly. Tutorea can be fighters, though they usually have others do their dirty work, if you will. I guess I have to keep using myself as an example. If you find a vampire breaking the rules, you would search out others of his kind and let them know so they can take care of it. It's more of an internal thing with each group."

"So I'm a narc now? What the fuck? That's so rude... I'm no tattle-tale."

"No, silly girl. You're a guardian. Again, without this, there would be chaos and things like the Inquisition: a very bad time to be a supernatural creature, I might add."

"Yeah but still... it's just so dirty." I shuddered at the thought.

"You could try to take care of the problem yourself, though you'd have a difficult time. I bet if we tried to arm wrestle, I'd win before you even gripped my hand."

"That's not very gentlemanly," I said

"I would say we need you, but I haven't seen the need for your kind in hundreds of years. Though I am still honored to meet you. After Melena, I never thought I'd see your kind ever again." He lifted my hand and gently kissed it.

"Really?" I asked, arching my brow.

"It's a sign of respect. Get over it."

I sighed. "If it helps, I can barely smell you now. I guess you really *are* a good boy, Rome."

"I should hope so. I haven't killed a man since 1789."

He followed me outside. "I suppose you don't have a car, huh?"

"Afraid not. I manage to get around without the need. However, I do like to take the train on occasion and people watch." He whistled and hailed a cab.

"I really shouldn't. I'm barely getting by with my shop—"

"Don't worry. I'll take care of it." He got in the cab with me and I gave the driver my address.

"Are you going to stalk me now that you know where I live?" I asked.

"Even if I were to, I can't come in without an invitation."

"Seriously? That little myth is true?"

"My dear girl, you have so much to learn. Perhaps I can tell you more another night."

"That would be helpful, thanks. I'm still not going to sleep with you."

"I wouldn't dare." He looked away.

Rome handed the driver a hundred. "Keep the change."

"Wow. Thanks, pal," the driver said glancing back at us. "Have a good night."

We got out of the cab and walked up to my porch.

"Lovely home," Rome said.

"Thank you. I'd invite you in but… even if you weren't a vampire, I still don't know you that well."

"Fair enough. I look forward to earning your trust." He backed up a bit and bowed.

"Well whatever you do, don't buy a trilby and start calling me 'm'lady.'"

He laughed again. "I wouldn't dare."

"Is that your catch phrase?"

"Maybe."

I unlocked my door and turned around to say goodbye, but he was already gone.

****

The phone inside the Mystery Box was ringing as soon as I walked in the door.

"Would you answer it already? Geez, that thing has been ringing all fuckin' morning," Frank said.

I picked up the phone. "Mystery Box, Onyx speaking."

"Onyx?"

"Lisbeth?"

"Yeah. Can I come by?"

"Sure. Why didn't you call my cell?"

"I lost mine and I couldn't find your number. Long story. I'll tell you when I get there."

I hung up with her.

"What's wrong with Liz?" Frank asked.

"I don't know."

Lisbeth arrived about an hour later. Like me, she had no access to a car and relied on her boyfriend to drive her around. Boyfriend being a relative term since he was always fucking around on her. She continued living with him in a "semi" relationship.

I was in my mid-twenties when I found myself in a similar setup so I understood how trapped a girl can feel in that type of situation.

She looked as though she had been crying.

"Oh man, what happened this time?" I asked.

"I have to be out by the end of the month... and I was fired today."

"When it rains it pours," I said with arms outstretched. "Come here." I walked around the counter and gave her a hug. "Well you'll always have a job here, with me. The pay is shit and I have no idea what I'm doing since I've never had an employee before… but you can be my assistant clerk."

"I'm not looking for handouts… and I don't want to impose—"

"Nonsense. Seriously, I've been needing someone for a while," I said.

"Really?" she asked.

"Yeah. You can start today if you like. I'll show you the ropes. Maybe we can even find you a place to live." As much as I adored her like the baby sister I never had, I refused to do the roommate thing. I couldn't fathom living with anyone I wasn't in a relationship with, and I avoided *those* like the plague.

She looked up at me with those big, anime eyes of hers. "It's basically stocking dildos, right?"

"Yeah… and rousting teenagers and the occasional pervert too."

Lisbeth was much tinier than me. She had a petite frame, completely flat on both ends and, I'm pretty sure, a natural blonde. Like me, she dyed her hair black and often wore corsets which gave her some semblance of a shape. Otherwise, between her perfect skin and innocent stare, she looked like a porcelain doll.

Half the time you wanted to squeeze the hell out of her to see if she made squeak sounds. It was hard to remember that she was an adult and not a twelve-year-old who stumbled onto her mother's retired punk gear and Siouxsie Sioux collection.

My cell phone rang; it was a local number I didn't recognize. "Hello?"

"Miss Mitchell?"

Oh hell no. "Sorry, you must have the wrong number."

"Onyx, I know this is your number."

"What do you want, Detective Stevens?" I asked, mildly annoyed that, not only did he say my name again, he stood me up as well.

"I wanted to apologize for not getting back to you yesterday. Something came up."

"Yeah well, it was rude and very unprofessional. It doesn't matter anyway. The ghost is not in the house anymore."

"What do you mean?" he asked.

"I went there last night and stayed for a few hours—"

"You went last night? Alone?"

"Um yeah. Anyway, nothing happened. I think whatever it is might be attached to something which was in the house. Have you spoken with Mr. Sanders or the kid?"

"Not today."

"Maybe I should head over there and talk—"

"Absolutely not. I don't want to frighten or put this family through any more trauma with this ghost nonsense that I'm not even sure *I* believe."

"Whatever," I said.

"It was against protocol to bring you into the house with me in the first place. I just wanted to tell you the case is in good hands and the Philadelphia Police Department no longer needs your assistance."

"Fine then. I didn't wanna help your ass anyway." I hung up.

"Who was that?" asked Lisbeth.

"Just some doughnut eating d-bag. Anyway, let me show you how I do restock orders."

Chapter 8

Onyx

There was no way I could let it go. I owed it to Mrs. Sanders to make sure her little girl was protected. If I hadn't failed in the first place, she might still be alive.

Remembering the address given to me by the moving guy, I took the bus to Mr. Sanders' house.

In the interest of not raising red flags, I dressed a little less Goth-heavy and kept my look more of an "angsty teenager's," especially if I had to pretend to be a babysitter—something of which might have proved interesting, considering I hadn't met the kid at all. I only knew her name from Mrs. Sanders' stories about her.

It was dinner time when I finally arrived at the Sanders' residence. I left Lisbeth in charge of the shop; it was her first test to see how everything would go without me there. Frank was under strict orders not to reveal himself. Though we weren't entirely sure of the consequences for spirits if they chose to reveal themselves or actively haunt your everyday human, he mostly kept to himself when the store was patronized by customers.

I rang the doorbell. Lily answered.

"Who are you?" she asked. It wasn't meant in a rude way, though kids seemed to have a very impolite way of speaking before they had a chance to learn otherwise.

I glanced behind her. "Listen, kid. I'm a friend of your mom's and I was helping her with your ghost problem. Just play along, okay?"

"Lily, I told you not to answer the door—hello," said a man who I assume was Mr. Sanders. "Can I help you?"

"Yeah. I was a friend of your ex-wife's. She hired me to babysit Lily on occasion." I gave Lily a look. "I was just dropping by to check on Lily."

He looked at his daughter. "Lily, do you know this girl?"

She looked at me then back to him. "Yeah. She babysits me."

"Alright well, come on in. We were just finishing up dinner. I can make you something if you'd like."

"Oh no... thank you. I ate already." Actually I hadn't. In fact, I was starving. "So Lily, did the movers bring you all your stuff from your mom's house?"

She frowned a bit and nodded.

Mr. Sanders spoke up. "The rest is in storage until I can have some sort of estate sale... perhaps I should just donate it."

"That would be great. Many of the shelters could always use furniture." One of the things I did before paranormal investigating was volunteer at the local woman's shelter. My appearance didn't go over big with some of the residents, and I was often mistaken for a runaway, so I had to find something else to occupy my time. "You had an awesome Hello Kitty collection there," I said to Lily, trying to cheer her up.

Lily looked up at me. "Do you like Hello Kitty?"

"I *love* Hello Kitty," I said.

She smiled. "Then I should show you the stuff I have here, there's even more." She grabbed my hand and led me up the stairs.

"If you guys need anything, I'll be down here," Mr. Sanders said from the foyer.

"So why did you have me lie to my dad?" Lily asked.

"I'm worried. Your mother hired me to rid the house of the ghost and I failed. I'm really sorry, Lily."

She nodded. "It's okay. Daddy said it was an accident... and not a ghost. He doesn't believe me."

"You haven't had any problems since, right?" I hoped whatever it was attached to might still be in the storage unit.

"Not until Monday… some of my toys will get moved around after I leave the room. And last night, it was really cold."

"Lily can you point out some of the things you had at your mom's?"

"Sure." She got up and walked to her closet. "Mostly just clothes and stuff on my dresser."

I pulled out my EMF and scanned some of the items she pointed to. Not a peep.

"What's that?" she asked.

"Oh this?" I waved the EMF a bit. "It just scans for ghosts. It tells me where they are hiding so I can pounce them." I made kitty claw gestures.

She giggled.

Her father walked in the room. "What are you doing?" he asked, seeing the EMF in my hands.

"Um…"

"Oh I know what this is. You're the girl my ex hired. I'm sorry but I'm going to have to ask you to leave. I don't want you filling Lily's head with this nonsense. She's scared enough as it is."

As soon as he stepped in, the EMF reader spiked.

"Does that mean the ghost is back?" Lily asked, running to her father's side.

"I don't know."

"That's it. I'm calling the cops." He pulled out his phone and dialed.

"Wait, seriously. Something isn't right and I know you don't believe me but I'm only trying to help your daughter, I swear."

"Yes, I have an intruder at 55 Terrace Avenue." He paused. "I'm not sure if she's dangerous, she just won't leave."

"Daddy, she's trying to help," Lily said.

I shot him a look.

"Yes, please hurry." He hung up. "Leave. Now."

"Fine! Don't say I didn't warn you." I sighed.

"Are you threatening us?" he asked.

"Daddy, look!" Lily pointed behind me and I saw a shadow hovering over a Hello Kitty doll.

"Lily, did that doll come from your mom's house?" I asked.

"Yeah, Annie gave it to me... she says it's a collector's item."

As I leaned in for a better look, she was indeed right: it was a first generation stuffed Hello Kitty doll to which I held up my EMF; it was spiking like crazy. I was an idiot not to have noticed it before—especially since it was a collector's item.

I tossed the EMF in my bag and picked up the doll with my index finger and thumb. "Get out of the way!" I called out as I ran passed them.

There was banging on the front door as I ran down the stairs. "Mr. Sanders? Open up. This is Detective Stevens."

I flung open the door and before Elliot could say anything, I pushed by him. "Out of the way! Haunted doll coming through." I tossed the doll on the grass and pulled out my salt and lighter fluid.

"What are you doing?" asked Mr. Sanders, yelling from behind me.

There was no time to answer anyone. I dumped the box of salt on the doll then doused it with lighter fluid before setting it ablaze. There was a giant green ball of fiery light which exploded causing me to fall back and everyone else to duck. A cloud of green smoke lingered for a moment before dissipating entirely.

"What the hell was that?" Elliot asked.

"The ghost."

"Why did you destroy my daughter's doll? You'll pay for that."

"Buddy, trust me. I feel worse about destroying that thing than you can possibly even know." I turned to Lily. "I'm sorry, kid. I promise I'll buy you another one." I looked back to Mr. Sanders. "So who is Annie and why did she give your kid that doll?"

"Anne is my fiancée and she found it at a yard sale. She's pretty good about finding antiques and collector's items."

A car pulled into the driveway and a woman got out in a frantic state. "Harry? What's going on?" She rushed over to Mr. Sanders and Lily.

"Apparently, you bought your step-daughter a haunted doll." I brushed my hands off before handing her my card. "So I hear you like to buy antiques. You should really be careful. If you ever acquire something questionable, I highly recommend you call me... just in case."

Elliot sighed. "Did you want to press charges?" he asked Mr. Sanders.

Lily ran over to me and hugged me. "Daddy, she got rid of the ghost."

Mr. Sanders looked at me for a moment, then his daughter. "Okay, sweetie." He looked back to Elliot. "No. Just... get her off my property."

I would have felt more offended if he didn't suffer a great loss already so I obliged without protest.

"Come on, Onyx," Elliot said as he reached for me.

Instinctively, I jerked back. "I'm out." I grabbed my bag and started walking away. I gave a quick wave "bye" to Lily.

Elliot said something to Mr. Sanders before running to catch up to me. "I knew you were the one he was calling about, you know. I had every intention of arresting you despite what Sergeant Longbear said."

"Whatever." I kept walking.

"Listen, I don't know what the hell happened back there and I really don't believe all... this, but if you really helped that family out—thanks."

I paused and looked at him. "You're thanking me? You know this case won't be solved unless you arrest some innocent guy."

"We're working with the M.E. on an accident theory... though I'm not supposed to be telling you that."

"Mum's the word. You can't even begin to know what kind of shit I have rattling around my brain which I can't speak a word of."

He looked at the house then back to me. "I don't doubt it."

I started walking again.

"Wait. At least let me give you a ride home."

"Actually, I need to go back to the shop. I left a new employee in charge so I could help out here, and I'm pretty sure I'll be coming back to a pile of rubble."

He laughed a bit. "You have no faith in people."

"It's not that. I just have more faith in the inevitable."

****

The store looked to be in pristine condition when we arrived.

I stepped inside to find Lisbeth with a very innocent and almost surprised look on her face. Like she had seen someone trip and was trying not to giggle.

The look instantly had me worried.

"Everything... okay?" I asked, looking around.

Elliot stopped just behind me.

Lisbeth's smile grew, which made her look even more doll-like. "Do you know you have a dead mobster haunting this place?" she asked in a mousey voice.

"God damn it, Frank," I muttered.

Elliot swallowed a bit and looked at me. Perhaps he didn't believe, but I could tell each clue was starting to win him over.

"He kept turning on the hardcore pornography and insisted he was allowed to watch it whenever."

"No, no he's not." I walked over to the counter and threw my bag behind it. "Other than the perverted ghost, anything else happen while I was away?"

"Yeah. I found an apartment. We only had one customer so I used the computer to look for one, is that okay?"

"Sure. Perfectly alright... and that's great."

Lisbeth looked at Elliot. "Who is this?"

"This is Detective Stevens. Detective Stevens... Lisbeth."

"Oh. Is this the doughnut eating d-bag you mentioned earlier?" Lisbeth asked.

I put my hand to my face.

"Doughnut... eating... d-bag. Really, Onyx?"

I sheepishly turned around to see Elliot arching a brow at me, a little bemused.

"I suppose I should get going," Elliot said.

"Nice meeting you," Lisbeth said in a chipper voice.

I couldn't say anything. If I was ever told my mouth would get me into trouble one of these days, today would be that day.

He stood there and looked at me for a moment before leaving.

"Damn."

"I'm sorry," Lisbeth said, obviously worried. "Sometimes I don't think before I speak."

The TV crackled a bit and I heard a boisterous echo of laughter booming through the speaker.

"This week needs to end, now," I said.

Chapter 9

Elliot

Onyx's obvious embarrassment was enough to cause me to chuckle, though I couldn't help but still feel attracted to her. Maybe ignoring her on Tuesday was a bad idea, it only made seeing her again that much more intense.

"You should have let me come with you and bust her," Nicki said as I stepped into the precinct.

"I knew it'd end up being nothing. I'm sure we won't be hearing from Mr. Sanders anymore."

"And why is that?"

"I don't believe this ghost business, but I saw some weird stuff tonight."

"We're cops, we see weird shit every night. I told you this would end up being a cold case."

"May I see you in my office?" Sergeant Longbear asked from his office door.

"Ooh, you're in for it now," Nicki said.

I sat in front of Sergeant Longbear's desk as he closed the door behind him.

"So what happened this evening? I noticed you left without your partner."

"It won't happen ag—"

He held up his hand. "That's not why I brought you in here. I believe Miss Mitchell is on our side. However, I want you to keep a close eye on her... from a distance, of course."

"I don't understand. Are you putting me on a stakeout?"

He chuckled. "Nothing of the sort. Just occasionally check up on her… see what she's up to, that sort of thing."

"May I asked why?" Why would Sergeant Longbear be so concerned with this girl when just the other night, he was telling me to work with her?

"Just as a precaution… for now. I'll expect updates weekly." He looked at his paperwork for a moment before lifting his eyes to me. "You'll be paid for your time." He looked back down again.

I took the gesture as my cue to leave.

"What was that about?" Nicki asked as I sat back down in my chair.

"Not sure, exactly."

On the way to my apartment, I swung by Onyx's house just in time to see her walking home. I maintained my distance and watched.

A man dressed in an overcoat approached her. From this distance, it looked as if she knew him. Odd he would be wearing an overcoat when it was seventy-five degrees out.

Onyx

"What do you want?" I asked as Rome approached me.

"Take care of your little ghost problem?"

"Yeah… I had to torch a doll older than me."

"Ah, the haunted porcelain doll. I've encountered those before," he said.

"Nah. Hello Kitty collector's plushy. It was totally depressing… now I have to find a replacement one for this kid or I'll be a doubly bad person."

"Why? You probably saved her and the rest of her family."

"Too late for her mother… I need to get her something at least."

"Don't beat yourself up. There was no way for you to know."

"That's the thing. I should have known… about all of it. Instead, I have to learn about my family history from some vampire… no offense."

"None taken. The offer still stands if you want to pick my brain for information."

"I'll take you up on it. Just not now" —I looked around— "and not here. Sorry, I still don't know you well enough to invite you inside."

"Understandably."

"So I guess the night is just beginning for you. Where are you off to next?"

"Nowhere really. I'm growing tired of Awakening."

"I hear ya. Actually, I'm starved. I should probably get something to eat. I really don't feel like cooking."

"I hear there's a lovely diner around the corner. My treat?" He gestured his hand behind him.

I laughed. "You don't even eat food… also, I'm not some charity case. I'm broke, but it's not *that* bad. Plus, I have a new employee now."

"Really?"

"Yeah, Lisbeth. My friend from the club. She got fired and her boyfriend kicked her out. Poor girl… *she's* the charity case."

He furrowed his brows. "Is that what she told you?"

"Yeah, why?" The look on his face worried me.

"No reason."

"No. You know something, what is it?" I asked.

"I just wasn't aware she had a boyfriend."

"Oh my God… you hooked up with her."

"No. Not in the least."

He definitely knew something and wasn't about to tell me what it was. "Should I be worried?" I asked.

"Not at all. Come on, you look paler than I do." He started walking.

If I were to get anything out of him, I'd have to play it cool. It seemed our all-revealing vampire had his fair share of secrets.

****

"Slow down there, girl. You're going to choke," Rome said.

"What are you, my mom now?" I asked with my mouth half full.

He laughed.

"I told you. I haven't eaten all day." I took another bite of my turkey burger.

He sat back and watched me.

"Stop that."

"Stop what?"

"Staring at me… it's creepy."

He said nothing and looked away.

"Do you miss eating real food?" I asked.

"It's been a while. I appreciate food for the art. In France in particular. They take food very seriously over there. Now, I appreciate it like one would a painting… maybe not this" —he picked up a fry then dropped it again— "exactly, but fine dining in general."

"I'm normally healthier than this. Killing a ghost seems to have made me crave greasy food." I shrugged. "Maybe killing a vampire would make me crave arty, expensive food," I said as I took another bite.

He smirked. "I don't know if you're brave or stupid. Although I can't imagine you get scared easily."

"I was a little freaked out at the thought of being alone with a ghost."

"I don't blame you. They make me uneasy as well. Something about the ethereal and the intangible. It's not like you can rip off its head or shoot it in the heart."

"The world isn't filled with ghosts, at least not that I've noticed. Why do you think some get trapped behind? Though behind from where is another question entirely."

"My guess is as good as yours. We can always go with the unfinished business theory. As for what happens to the rest of us... I've seen many people die over the centuries and I still don't have an answer to that question. All there is, is this life."

"Unless you find a way to cheat death," I said with a grin.

"Touché."

"Aren't you bored of it all yet? Not to sound cliché, but you must have seen the worst of mankind and generations of people not learning the lessons of the past."

"That's pretty astute of you. Perhaps it's why I stick around. Occasionally I encounter interesting people such as yourself... and Melena."

"Were you in love with her?" I asked.

"Why do you ask?"

"You keep bringing her up. I notice I tend to talk about ex-lovers I have unresolved issues with, more than I should."

"Yes. I was. I suppose I still am. She was a woman before her time."

"If she is an ancestor of mine, I don't doubt she was," I said.

"To answer your question, there have been times throughout my life, I wanted to end it all. Existing felt monotonous and pointless. One of those times was just after she died."

"What made you stick around?"

"I suppose the idea of love itself. She wasn't the first, nor was she the last, but she made the biggest impression on me. I suppose I loved her the most."

"That's sweet."

He smiled but I could see the sadness in his eyes.

I couldn't imagine living an extended period of time and dealing with loss over and over again. I could barely hold myself together after my aunt died. My mother was a different story entirely. I feared her before she met her untimely death probably because she was such a Jesus-freak, though my aunt told me that wasn't always the case. It was only after my father left that she turned out that way.

"What are you thinking about?" he asked.

"My mother... I guess. It just popped in there."

"What happened to her? If I may ask."

"I suppose it's only fair I tell you since you've told me your life story... at least part of it. She died when I was nine. My aunt pretty much raised me. All I knew is that she was sick though it was never revealed to me what caused her death exactly. The last time I saw her was in the hospital. She said she was being punished for her sins." I shook my head. "I really don't want to talk about it."

He reached over and rested his hand over mine. Once again, it went from clammy to warm within a few seconds.

I pulled my hand back. "It wasn't an invitation for you to find out more. I don't even want to think about it."

"I see what you mean," he said. I'm pretty sure he caught a glimpse of what was in my mind's eye.

The bell over the diner door rang and I turned around just in time to see Elliot walking in.

"Oh fuck me, really?" I said as I snapped my gaze forward again.

"Who is that?" Rome asked in a hushed tone.

"The cop I mentioned before."

Rome looked past me again and smirked a bit. "He's quite handsome."

"What? Do you like guys or something?" I asked.

"You don't live as long as I do and *not* sample all life has to offer."

"Whoa. Slow down there, Casanova. I'm pretty sure he's straight." I looked over my shoulder again and saw Elliot narrow his eyes a bit as he walked over toward us.

Rome leaned into the corner of the booth and windowed wall with his arm propped up on the table. "Good evening, officer."

Perhaps Elliot caught the flirtation in Rome's voice since he sat next to me instead of him. "Hello."

Rome sat up a bit and extended his hand. "Rome."

Elliot met his hand. "Detective Elliot Stevens. Rome... got a last name?"

"Son of William."

I choked on my iced tea. "So, Elliot. What can I help you with?" I asked while clearing my throat.

"Nothing. Just here for a bite to eat."

"Really? Just randomly picked this diner for no reason?" I asked in disbelief.

He didn't answer though it was clear he was thinking something as he stared at Rome. "Got any ID?"

I looked at Rome. "You're not legally obligated to show him," I said. I turned back to Elliot. "What's this about?"

"Perhaps I should leave you two alone," Rome said as he moved to get up.

"No. You don't have to go anywhere." I looked at Elliot again. "Explain yourself."

Still, Elliot said nothing. His expression was a little grim as if he regretted coming in here in the first place.

"Fine then. Get out of my way," I said.

"No. Please," Rome said as he shifted to the edge of the booth. "I should be going." He took my hand and gave it a kiss before sliding out of the booth. "Also, don't worry about the check."

"Oh come on," I said as he was leaving. I looked at Elliot again. "What's your problem, man?"

"Who was that?" Elliot asked.

"A friend."

"From where?"

"Are you interrogating me about my friends now? Not that it's any of your business, but if gets you to go away, fine: he's someone from the club. He's a history buff and I was asking about some things."

"About what exactly?"

"About, I don't know... the history of haunted dolls." I moved to get up, but he wouldn't budge. He just stared at me. Almost as if he caught me cheating on him. *Wait.* "Oh I see what this is—you're jealous."

He swallowed and got out of the booth.

Bingo. I grabbed my things and stood up. "Leave Rome alone. He's just a friend, not that it should be any concern of yours. I mean, why are you even following me? I assume that's what you were doing."

He closed his eyes and kept silent.

"Ugh." I walked out of the diner and headed home.

Elliot

You're an idiot. You should have just stayed in the car and waited.

"Rome," I said to myself as I sat back in the car and pulled out my tablet. *No one with the alias Rome…* which made me even more curious as to who he was. Something about him made me uneasy. He was also acting awfully friendly with Onyx.

There was no way I could bring Nicki on my after-hours stakeout; I knew she'd object or interfere in some way, and her being my partner for less than a year, we still had yet to develop a bond. She could instinctually read me when things got violent, and she physically had my back better than any other partner I've had in the past, but when it came to social graces, she was pretty lacking.

As far as partners go, I wouldn't trade her for any other. Anyone who spoke twice about women on the force quickly changed their minds after meeting Nicki Alcott.

My first night watching Onyx and I had already blown it. The best option now would be to back off for about a week and let my presence become a faded memory. The thought had me sad for a moment.

My cell phone's ring tone snapped me back to attention.

"Detective Stevens," I answered.

"Hey buddy." I could hear loud noises in the background as if Nicki was at a bar or some other crowded place.

"Hello, Nicki."

"You off work yet? I swear, you're like teacher's pet."

"Yes, I'm off. About to head home, actually."

"Why don't you come join me for a drink?"

"It's the middle of the week. Why are you drinking?" The last thing I needed was to deal with a hung-over partner in the morning.

"Rough day."

Odd. I'd spent nearly all day with her and it hadn't seemed rough to me. "Um, sure."

"I'm at Jackson's on Fifth."

I sighed and hung up the phone. *I'm going to regret this.*

"Hey, partner!" *Yup.* She was drunk.

I walked over and sat across from her in the booth. "What's going on?"

"Just got a phone call tonight. My ex is getting married." She downed a shot.

The only breakup which affected me was with my ex-fiancée, and even that was somewhat amicable. In this case, I couldn't really relate to Nicki. "I'm sorry to hear that." I looked at the row of empty shot glasses. "And you think *this* is a good idea?"

"Yup." She belched.

"Alright, I'm taking you home." I stood up.

"No way! You just got here."

"Listen, I've had a pretty annoying night myself and I can safely say, what we both need right now is sleep." I glanced at my watch. "It's still early enough for you to go to bed and still be able to function tomorrow."

"Boo. Why are you such a goody-two-shoes? They would have eaten you alive at my last post." She stood up and stumbled a bit.

I quickly grabbed her and put her arm around my shoulder for balance.

"Gettin' kinna close there, Ellie." She snickered.

I shook my head. "Come on."

"We'll have to come back for your car tomorrow," I said as we pulled away.

She looked out the window seemingly in thought... or she could have just been trying to steady her gaze on something. "So what happened to you tonight that was so bad?"

"Just ran into someone. Hey, back at your old position... ever run into a guy named Rome?"

She closed one eye. "Hmm... nope. Can't say that I have. I've heard the name Romoalt... but that was back when I first started. Don't think it's the same guy though."

"Unusual name."

"This is an unusual town."

"That it is," I said.

We pulled up to her apartment.

"Wanna tuck me in, officer?" she asked with a devious grin.

"Goodnight, Nicki. I'll pick you up tomorrow," I said while looking forward. The last thing I needed was to make eye contact and have her do something stupid like try to kiss me.

"You're no fun." She slammed the door and stomped toward the lobby of her building.

I was two for two tonight with the ladies. These days, it was easier to talk to victims and families of victims than it was women.

Chapter 10

Onyx

I wasn't bothered by Elliot's actions as much as the mysterious statement made by Rome about Lisbeth. It was common knowledge about Lisbeth and her tumultuous relationship with her boyfriend Dave. He frequented the club back when Lisbeth was a waitress, and ended up getting her fired after he kept threatening nearly every guy she took a drink order from.

Dave got 86'd and Lisbeth lost her job. If she decided to stop going, I'd completely understand... but this was two years ago and she still goes to Awakening as if nothing has changed.

I'd seen Dave once since that night, about six months ago, when he screamed at her as she was leaving his house to meet me out front. Lisbeth's most recent job was waitressing at a strip club with Friday nights off so she could spend them at the club with me.

She was still with Dave then... and Rome started appearing at the club around a month ago. Maybe Lisbeth was involved with him somehow. They both did well to act otherwise the first night I met him.

****

The next day, Lisbeth was standing just outside the shop as I walked up.

"You're early," I said.

"Just want to make a good impression," she replied.

"I would never doubt you a hard worker... I suppose I never actually gave you hours, huh?"

"Nope," she said in her cute, mousey voice.

"I guess we can work on that today. Thursdays are boring as shit." I unlocked the door and tossed my bag behind the counter. "My basic opening is this: I unlock the door, flip the sign, check the phone messages and email, then restock based on whatever was dropped off in the delivery room. Now that you're here, you can... check the delivery room, I guess."

"Right-o, boss." She walked toward the back room, practically skipping.

"Are you sure she's even eighteen?" asked Frank.

"I know right? She's just so tiny. I want to put her in a glass case and keep her for display purposes only. But no, she's twenty-two."

"Yeesh. Kids these days."

I skimmed through my emails. They were mostly requests for specific toys or brands and new releases based on production companies. The phone messages were another story.

"I know what you are," said a breathy whisper before I heard a click.

"Who the fuck was that?" asked Frank.

"Dude, I don't know. What a creeper."

"Who's a creeper?" asked Lisbeth who was walking toward me with an armful of packaged dildos.

I couldn't help but giggle. "Now I know what *I* look like restocking."

She looked down for a moment before laughing herself. "There were two boxes, should I just look for where to put these?"

"Yeah, most orders are things I've run out of or plan to run out of. Dildos are straight back, vibrators are to the right, and lube is in the center case. Just leave the DVD's. I think that should be all of it."

"Okie dokie." She went back to restock.

"Should I just give her the same schedule as me? And have her stay if I have to run off for an errand?"

"She's too frail to work alone at night. There's only so much I can do," Frank said.

I glanced around the corner just in time to see her struggling to slide a package on a hook while on her tippy toes. "I guess I'll just have her work when I do. That's really going to cut into the minimal profits I make as is."

"Look at it this way, you're doing a good deed."

I suppose Frank was right, but I still needed a plan to generate more business. Paranormal investigating wasn't going to cut it when it came to my own personal bills at home.

Lisbeth walked back over to the counter. "Do we have a step ladder anywhere?"

I giggled. "Yes. It's in the back. Wait. Can I ask you something?"

"Sure."

"What happened with Dave exactly? I understand if you don't want to talk about it."

"I guess I just couldn't take his temper anymore. Plus losing my job was a great motivator to get out."

There was another question. "What happened at the strip club?"

"They were making all the waitresses dance, and you know I'm not down with that."

"I don't blame you, not that anyone would judge if you did," I said.

"I know. I had a little money stashed away which is why I'm able to pay for this studio apartment... plus I have an income again. How much am I getting paid exactly?"

"Oh yeah. I still have to figure that out, but you'll be paid weekly."

She smiled. "Thanks."

My phone beeped with a text from George: *Awakening closed. Someone got killed last night.*

I quickly pulled up the local news on the store's computer. "Oh shit."

"What is it?" Lisbeth asked.

"Someone died at Awakening."

"What? When?"

"Last night," I said.

She walked behind the counter and peered at the screen. "No shit…"

"Says here it was a young girl… her body was found mutilated in the alley behind the club. That's a fucked up way to go." Something about it didn't seem right either.

"Do you think they'll be open by tomorrow night?" Lisbeth asked.

"Lisbeth! Wow."

She held up her hands in defense. "It was just a question."

Regardless, I'd have to check it out at some point… just in case.

Chapter 11

Elliot

"Any leads on that mutilation at Awakening?" asked Sergeant Longbear.

"Not yet," I replied.

He didn't immediately leave. "The location is interesting, don't you think?"

"If you're asking if our mutual friend might be involved, I highly doubt it. You forget, I can account for her whereabouts last night." I was mildly annoyed at the implications though it brought up questions about Onyx's mystery friend, Rome.

"The owners insist on reopening tomorrow night. They seem to have friends in high places. Perhaps you should go down there and… observe."

"Observe what?" Nicki asked as she approached.

"Your partner will fill you in," Sergeant Longbear said as he walked away.

I stared in his direction for a moment before addressing Nicki. "Feeling better?"

"Oh… yeah. I have a mother of a headache but coffee helps." She lifted her mug.

"We're going to keep an eye on Awakening tomorrow night."

"Ooh fun. It'll give me an excuse to bust out my combat boots."

"I highly doubt we'll be going inside."

"Too bad."

****

I was tempted to call Onyx though I was sure she had heard the news by now. If I saw her, I wasn't sure if I could keep from approaching her.

"This is going to be boring. Why can't we just go inside? At least there's music."

I kept an eye on the alley way. "We wouldn't want to spook any would-be perps, now would we?" I asked.

She chuckled quietly. "Hey, isn't that your little ghost hunting girlfriend?"

There she was… as pale and gorgeous as ever. I glared at Nicki for a moment before looking back at Onyx. She was with her friend Lisbeth.

"Sure you don't want to go in *now*?" Nicki asked, tauntingly.

"No. We are staying here." Just as I said the words, I saw Rome enter the club and I moved to open the car door.

"Wait. I thought you just said we're staying here?"

"I've changed my mind."

"You can't go in looking like that." She cocked a brow as she looked me up and down.

I just rolled my eyes and shook my head.

"No… ugh. Stop." She leaned forward and slipped off my blazer before unbuttoning the top two buttons of my shirt and taking off my tie.

"What are you doing?" I asked.

"It's a good thing the rest of your outfit is black. Look at that place. No one is going to talk to someone who obviously looks like a cop." She sat back a moment. "I guess this will have to do. You're way too clean cut for this place."

"And what do you know of it?"

"I frequented places like this back in the day," she said with a grin.

"Well for right now I need you to keep an eye on the alley way."

"What? I'm not coming with you?" she asked.

"One of us needs to stay here and I see someone I need to speak to."

"'Someone.'" She shot me a look. "So you're going in there… without backup."

"It's just a quick questioning. I'll be back shortly."

"Ugh, fine. Wait." She ran her fingers through my hair and messed with it a bit. "Just go… you're hopeless."

Rather than alert the bouncer at the door that I was a cop, I flashed him my ID instead of my badge upon entering. As soon as I stepped in, I saw Onyx sitting at the bar with her friend; Rome was leaning over her from behind, whispering something into her ear. She laughed and I instantly felt angry.

She seemed startled as I approached. "Elliot? What the hell are you doing here?"

I glanced at Lisbeth then Rome. "I'm here about the murder on Wednesday night."

"I don't know anything about it. Some poor girl got killed. Sucks," said Onyx.

"And you're not worried the same could happened to you?" I glanced to Rome again to which he responded in a questioning expression.

"No. I can take care of myself. Isn't it a little late to be questioning people?" Onyx asked.

"Where were you?" I asked Rome.

Onyx glanced at Rome then back to me. "It wasn't him, I can guarantee you that."

"Oh? And how is that?"

She cleared her throat. "I was with him all night… and before that, you saw both of us."

I immediately knew she was lying though she seemed pretty confident about him not doing it. "I have a few questions for you, Rome."

He smiled. "Anything I can do to help. Shall we?" He motioned for me to follow him to the back.

Onyx got up.

"You stay here," I said.

"The hell I will," Onyx said.

"Want me to cuff you and toss you in the back of my car again?"

Lisbeth giggled. "Kinky."

She wasn't half wrong. An image of Onyx handcuffed naked to my bed flashed in my thoughts.

"Whatever," Onyx said before sitting back down.

I followed Rome as he led me to a quiet booth.

"Now," he said while sitting," what questions did you have for me, Detective?"

I sat across from him. "What's your relationship with Onyx?"

He narrowed his eyes slightly before smirking. "I thought you were here to find out about that poor girl's murder?"

He was right. *Why did I ask him that?* "How often do you come to Awakening?" I asked.

"Nearly every night it's open."

"See anything unusual recently?"

"It's a Goth club, I see 'unusual' all the time."

As I watched him, he seemed to study my face. Almost like he was making bedroom eyes at me. I cleared my throat. "Had you seen the victim around?"

"No. And I know most of the regulars. She wasn't one of them. I'm curious, Detective, why are you questioning me out of all these people here?"

"I'll get to them soon enough. After I saw you Wednesday night, where did you go?"

"Home."

"Miss Mitchell said she was with you all night; are you refuting her alibi?"

"I didn't kill anyone… though I can't say the same for the man who did should I get my hands on him. I abhor violence against women." His playful gestures and expression turned serious in an instant.

"So you went home... and where is that exactly? It would be nice to get a full name as well."

His smile returned for a moment. "189 Wicker Drive. Romoalt William... son."

The address put him in Gladwyne, an extremely wealthy suburb of Philadelphia... and the name: Romoalt... Nicki had specifically mentioned that name when I asked her about his alias. "Can anyone account for your whereabouts at your residence?"

"Just the ghosts in the walls... I hear you have experience with those."

I glared at him. "Do me a favor and don't leave town anytime soon." I moved to get up.

He brought his hand to mine. "Don't you want me to answer your first question, Detective?"

"It's not relevant to this investigation." I moved my hand.

"But it *is* relevant to you. Onyx and I are just friends... recent acquaintances actually. She's quite special, that one."

I wanted to ask what he meant by that, but the way he looked at me was making me uneasy, it was mildly predatory.

Onyx was downing a shot as I approached her.

"I take it you have questions for me too?" she asked.

"No." I shot Rome a look before leaving.

"Wait," she called out as we both exited the club. "What the hell was that about?"

"I just had questions for your friend."

"And no one else? That's some shoddy police work if you ask me."

"How I do my job is none of your concern."

"The hell it isn't. My taxes pay your salary, pal." She jabbed her fingers in my chest.

Nicki approached us in a slight jog. "Problem here, Elliot?"

"No problem."

"Oh look, it's K-9 cop," Onyx said with a chuckle.

"That's it." Nicki stepped on the curb and stood in front of Onyx.

"Nicki, calm down. She's clearly drunk."

"Oh goody. She's outside of the club, we can bust her for public intoxication."

I put my hands on her shoulders and pushed her back a bit. "No. We're not going to do anything except get back in the car and leave."

"You're fucking lucky he likes you," Nicki said, pointing a finger at Onyx.

I moved to grab Nicki but she slapped my hand away and stormed off.

"Seriously, bro. You need to invest in a dog whistle or something."

The dog references were borderline unusual though I could only imagine they were some sort of insult with purpose. Whatever it was, it was working; Nicki was mad.

"Goodnight, Onyx."

"Goodnight, *detective*," Onyx said.

Nicki was fuming by the time I got back to the car.

"One of these fucking days, man. I'm going to clock that bitch."

"Calm down, Nicki. Don't forget, *you're* the professional," I said.

"Back at my old job, I could do anything I wanted. I ate girls like her for breakfast."

Onyx

"So why did he come here to question one person?" Lisbeth asked.

"Because he's an asshole and a shitty cop," I sighed, "and a mood killer. I was so looking forward to someone going down on me tonight, too."

Lisbeth giggled.

"You can still have that if you wish," Rome whispered in my ear as he ran his hands over my shoulders.

There was no way I'd go down that road with Rome, no matter how tempting the offer was. As much as Elliot pissed me off, I still wanted him and it frustrated the hell out of me.

"I can make that happen too," Rome continued. "Though it wouldn't take much. He wants you so bad it actually clouds his judgment. I saw it for myself."

"Get out of my head you dirty old man."

"Just trying to help."

"I hope you don't use those 'skills' of yours to coerce women into hooking up with you. You know that's rape, right?"

"I have not. But I do use it as motivation if I sense something is already there. It's not difficult these days."

"Seriously?" I asked in mild annoyance.

"Women's liberation has worked well for both genders," he said with a devious grin. He looked to Lisbeth who was innocently staring off at the crowd on the dance floor.

"I'm sorry, Rome, but I have to ask—did you have anything to do with that girl being killed?"

"I'm insulted you would entertain the thought. Absolutely not. Besides, if I harmed another living soul, you'd know in an instant."

"How do I know you aren't lying about that?"

"Would you like me to hurt someone just to prove it?" he asked.

"No—"

"Then I suggest you accept my answer as truth. I have no reason to lie."

"You could. I still don't know you, not really. Just because you shared your life history doesn't make us friends."

He scowled at me and grabbed my hand before dragging me out the back door.

"Where are you taking me?" I demanded.

Once the door closed behind us, he released his grip and stared at me.

"What?" I asked.

Something in his eyes changed; like a dark cloud passing over a deep blue ocean. He lunged forward and grabbed me, biting into my neck.

I screamed. It slowly faded into a moan.

He stopped after a few seconds.

Almost instantly, the smell of garbage emanated from him. I backed away in disgust while holding my neck. "What the fucking fuck?!"

"Now do you see? I told you the truth and I want you to be able to trust me... as a friend."

"So you intentionally bit me to prove you're my friend? What the hell sense does that make?" I removed my hand and looked at the blood. "That's gonna leave a mark."

"Here. Allow me." He stepped forward; I instinctively moved back. "I swear I will never harm you again... not even to prove a point."

"Fine. You get one chance with me, got it?"

"I completely understand and agree. You should know, though, what I'm about to do is against the rules." He bit into his thumb and ran his blood over my neck.

I felt a warmth before reaching up and touching the area. He had healed the puncture marks. "What? Your blood heals people? Why aren't you in a hospital curing cancer or something—holy shit."

"I told you. It's against the rules. We're not allowed to interfere with the fabric of humanity."

"Did someone tell that to the guy who made you?" I asked.

"I told you. The rules have changed over the years. You're different. Here's hoping there aren't any consequences."

"It's not a huge deal... it would have healed in a week I guess." I touched my neck again.

He leaned down and licked the rest of the blood off my neck, then my hand. "Might I add how delicious you taste?"

"Probably better than you smell right now. Ugh."

"It'll go away eventually, though this time it might take longer." He seemed a little saddened by this revelation... as was I. "There are many things you still need to learn. I suppose this can be your first official lesson. Perhaps next time you'll believe me and not question my intentions."

"Do you blame me? You're a vampire... whatever truth you know, lore says I should be running for my life. You're lucky I let you get this far."

He narrowed his eyes and glanced over his shoulder.

"What—"

He held up his hand, motioning for me to be silent.

Seconds later, there was a loud scream from further down the alley. "Who was that?"

In an instant, he ran off toward the direction of the scream. Based on the first night we talked, it didn't surprise me he was able to move so quickly, but seeing it was something else altogether. I snapped from my thoughts and took off after him.

I caught up to him just in time to see him standing over the body of a girl. She didn't look like someone who frequented Awakening.

"Holy shit."

"I didn't get here in time... though I did see something take off very fast."

"Like *your* kind of fast? Or just ran off?"

"My kind of fast... it wasn't a vampire. A vampire wouldn't do something like this," he said, pointing toward the large gashes across her torso.

I could have felt sick by seeing a dead body mangled in such a way, but I was more intrigued than anything. "What do you think it was?"

"I'm not sure. Do you smell anything?"

I sniffed the air. "I smell her perfume... trash... which is probably you, or the alley," I said looking around. "Wait. Burning.

Kind of like… I don't know. I don't want to say burning wood, because that's what Sergeant Longbear smelled like and it isn't that."

"You're going to have to train that nose of yours," he said.

"Why? It's not like I have anything to compare it to. I only know a handful of scents and that's because my aunt described them to me."

"I may have a way to get you some resources… however, for now, we need to figure out what's going on here."

"I should call Elliot… which means you should skedaddle."

"I'm not going anywhere… besides, I've been with you all night." He smirked at me.

"Ugh, don't remind me." I pulled out my phone and dialed the last number Elliot called me from.

"Detective Stevens."

"Elliot?"

"Onyx?"

"Are you still at Awakening?"

"No. I left after we spoke, why?"

"There's been another attack. It's further down the alley from where the last girl was killed."

"Don't move, I'll be right there. And don't touch *anything*." He hung up.

"Guess we're staying here."

"Hey where have you guys been?" Lisbeth said as she ran over to us. "What's that—oh my God!" She screamed.

"Lisbeth, calm down." I ran over to her and held her. "It's okay."

Moments later, Elliot arrived with his partner.

"What happened? Did you touch anything?" Elliot asked. He glared at Rome for a second.

"Rome and I were in the alley behind Awakening, talking, when we both heard a scream and ran over here."

"Talking, huh? Did you see anything when you got here?"

"No, just a body." I looked at Rome.

"Whatever did this has claws," said Rome.

"And how would you know that?" asked Elliot.

Rome moved to speak when Lisbeth stepped closer, looking at the body. "I know her."

"What?" I asked.

"Yeah, she used to work at the club until she got fired, this was before I was let go."

Elliot pulled out his notepad. "What's her name?"

"Alisha. I don't remember her last name, sorry. You can probably find out more from the owner," Lisbeth said.

More officers began to arrive, including Sergeant Longbear. "What's she doing here?" he asked Elliot.

"She was the one who found the body," Elliot said.

"I see."

Elliot pulled up a picture on his phone and walked over to Lisbeth. "Do you know this girl?"

It was a picture of the girl who died Wednesday night.

"Yeah, but she didn't work at the club. I used to see her about once a month. Is this the first girl?" Lisbeth asked.

"Yes. Have you seen anyone or anything odd in relation to these two women?"

"No. Like I said, the last time I saw Alisha was almost a year ago."

"If you think of anything else, please call me," Elliot said before giving me a quick glance. His gaze moved to my neck. "Are you injured?"

I realized there was some dried blood on my neck from earlier. "No. Makeup snafu."

"The same applies to you. If you think of anything, call me." He looked over to Rome a moment before walking back over to Sergeant Longbear.

"You three can leave," said Sergeant Longbear.

I nodded and walked away with my arm around Lisbeth. Rome took a few seconds before joining us.

"What do you think this is?" I asked Rome.

"I'm not sure. Claw marks like those can come from any number of creatures, even wild animals."

"I highly doubt a wild animal is stalking and slashing Goth girls," I said as we walked. "That partner of Elliot's is a werewolf; think it could have been one of those?"

"Possibly, though they leave behind a much gorier mess as well as eat vital organs." He looked at Lisbeth then to me. "Is it wise to be talking about such things in the open?"

"Don't worry about me. Nothing surprises me… also, the Mystery Box is haunted."

"So I've heard. Still. Onyx… you really should watch what you say, there are still rules—"

"What rules? You keep mentioning these rules… my aunt talked about them, yet I haven't seen anything that explains what they are or where they came from. And fuck the rules if they aren't enforced when things like this happen." I glanced back over my shoulders. "Seriously," —I stopped— "give me an example of the rules being enforced."

"The witch trials… the Inquisition… need I go on?"

I looked at Lisbeth. "You won't say anything, right?"

"Of course not. I think this stuff is neat… except when people get hurt. Wait so… what are you?" she asked Rome before looking at me.

"It's a long story," I said as I glanced over my shoulder. "We should get out of here before they ask more questions we can't answer."

"Are we going to your house?" asked Lisbeth.

I looked at Rome. "Let's just go to the shop."

Chapter 12

Onyx

"So that was Sergeant Longbear?" Rome asked.

"Yup."

"Interesting. I don't believe I've ever seen a wendigo before... then again, I can't point them out like you can."

"Who's this?" Frank asked through the static on the TV. Rome looked around in alert.

"That's our friendly ghost. Frank, meet Rome. Rome, Frank."

"Ah. Italy! My family's from Rome."

Rome chuckled. "You weren't kidding about the ghost."

"Nope," Lisbeth said in her traditional squeak-like manner. "All he does is watch porn all day."

Rome laughed harder. "Is that so?"

"You say this like it's a bad thing. What else am I supposed to do, trapped in this shop all damn day?"

"He earns his keep, so-to-speak, by scaring any potential thieves during the off hours. As long as he's not blasting it while I'm working, I don't really care."

"Fair enough," Rome said. He took a quick look around the shop. "Ever thought about staying open after nine?"

"No way. I already devote my life to this place. Why? Need a job?" I asked, arching a brow.

"No. I just wondered. Most of my nights are spent at Awakening... and *other places*."

"What *other places*?" I asked.

"There are other more secret clubs...and the occasional swingers club." He smiled.

"And that's all you're going to say on the matter?"

"Exactly."

"Tell me, have you been a whore your entire life? Or is this just a recent development," I asked in a reporter-tone voice.

"Why couldn't I be stuck in one of those places?" Frank asked.

"I would say recent development, though recent for me is different for you."

"I'll bet." I thought a moment. "We probably should have gone to my house. All of the books my aunt left me are there... not that they'd tell me anything new. I've read them cover to cover."

"Do you have the internet here?" Rome asked.

"Yes. Why? I thought most of what's online is bullshit as far as supernatural myth and mystery go."

"Not all of it. Not if you know where to look."

I turned on my computer and logged in. "Have at it, buddy."

"Have you heard of Tor?"

"Dark net? The place where hackers go to jerk off to donkey porn and financial transaction packet sniffing? Maybe."

"There are a few domains dedicated to documenting the supernatural. It's a way for our world to police itself. Like I said, I haven't seen someone like you in nearly 500 years."

"Holy shit, you're a vampire!" Lisbeth perked up. "I knew it! I told Onyx you were too good looking for that douche crowd."

"Some of the best vampire movies came out in the seventies... like 'Blacula,'" Frank said.

I laughed. "Yup, that's a good one."

"I'm afraid I have not seen it," said Rome.

"I'm sure I can dig it out somewhere. I prefer zombie movies." I pressed the power button of the TV. "Sorry Frank, you're going to have to haunt the stereo." Before Frank could protest, I turned on "Night of the Living Dead."

Frank groaned. "Can't you play something else?"

"Fine." I took out the tape and pushed in "Evil Dead."

"Better?"

"Why can't you put on some of those horror movies where the girls are always topless before they die?"

I just shook my head. "Find anything?" I asked Rome.

"Well if we exclude wendigos and werewolves, there aren't many creatures who would venture this far into an urban environment. I posted something on the forums. Maybe someone will get back to me." He uploaded a picture.

"What, you took a picture? That's sick."

"I needed to or we'd get nowhere. This isn't for my amusement. Any unexplained murders, or events which shine a light into our world, is extremely bad for business." He closed the browser. "Now. What shall we do next?"

"You mentioned something about having some more information for me?"

"Yes... I have some things back at my place."

"Can I see them?" I asked.

"That depends. I don't think I know you well enough to allow you into my home."

"Oh don't play that card with me, pal."

"It's still early. You're both welcome to join me," he said, eyeing Lisbeth.

It occurred to me that maybe they were both hiding something from me.

"I think I'll pass. I should head home," Lisbeth said.

"I don't feel good about you walking home at this hour. We can share a taxi," I said.

"Nah. I got it. See ya tomorrow," she said before leaving.

I furrowed my brows. "Something is going on with her... and you," I said as I turned back to Rome.

"What do you mean?"

"You keep giving her suggestive looks. Are you trying to bed my best friend?"

"I wouldn't dare."

"Right."

"She's seen and heard a lot tonight. Despite what she says, no one just slides into our world unscathed. She may need to absorb it."

"Perhaps you're right. Anyway. I know you can take two steps and be at your front door, but I need a ride."

"Of course." He picked up the phone and called a cab. "Don't worry, I'll pay for it," he said with a smile.

"I didn't say anything," I said.

"I know what you're thinking."

I looked down at my hands; he wasn't touching me.

"Your expression, silly girl. You can be quite obvious."

I rolled my eyes and sighed.

****

As the cab went further away from the city, the homes grew larger. "Where do you live exactly?" I asked.

"You'll see."

The way he looked at me and the tone of his voice worried me.

The cab finally pulled up to a gate and rolled far enough in for Rome to enter a code from the back seat.

Judging from the size of the gate, I was right to feel worried.

"Ho-ly shit," I said as I got out of the cab.

The house was massive... more like a manor.

Rome handed the driver some money. "Keep the change."

The driver smiled. "Thanks, man."

"How generous of you," I said as the cabbie drove off.

"There's no point in hoarding money. Besides, what I value most is inside." He entered a code and opened the front door, motioning for me to enter.

The opulence was far more intimidating than I ever viewed Rome to be. "Is this a house or a museum?" I asked as I walked toward a marble bust. "How old is this stuff?"

"Some of it is very old, others... not so much. These are just things I've collected over the centuries."

"I love how you say that so casually, as if that's the norm." I continued to look around. "How can you afford a place like this? Even if you had a job... this is some serious money."

"You're right. I've invested wisely over the years, sold a few pieces I might have acquired from less than reputable ways."

"How much money do you have?" I asked before realizing it was a rude question. "Sorry. I shouldn't—"

"It's quite alright. And to be honest, I don't actually know. It's invested all over the world, and housed in a few international banks. The changes in tax laws over the years have made it easier for me to increase my wealth so I try to give back where I can."

"Oh yeah... those assholes on Wall Street trying to ruin the country could learn a thing or two from your example."

"Exactly. My position has me benefitting from the changes made by the extremely wealthy... but it's not how I choose to exist in this world."

"I guess that's something to be admired. So where are these books of yours?" I asked.

"Straight to business, I see. Very well then, follow me." He led me to a hidden door behind the stairs.

"Are you taking me to a sex dungeon?"

He burst out laughing. "No. Though I do have one."

I perked up a bit. "Really?"

"Would you prefer to see that instead?"

Of course I wanted to, but I couldn't say that without giving Rome the wrong idea. "Um... no. Let's just get to the books."

The room looked like something from a horror flick involving a mad professor. There was antique science equipment everywhere as well as a library of books. In this case, I would call them tomes. "You're kidding right?"

"What?" Rome looked around.

"This is more like a Hollywood set than a real place. Where the hell did you find all this?"

"Most of it is stuff I bought brand new. I told you, I've collected over the years."

"More like hoarded." I picked up an old flask. "Seriously, I meet my first vampire and he's a hoarder." I set it down and wiped my fingers off on my skirt. "You need a maid."

"No one comes down here. *I* rarely come down here." He walked over to the bookshelf and pulled out a few. "Go through these and see if you can find out anything relevant to what you're aunt told you. We'll expand from there."

As soon as I opened the first book, I knew there was no way. "I don't speak Latin or... whatever this other language is."

"That, my dear, is Basque."

"And you speak it?"

"Yes. I speak over thirty languages." He thought for a moment. "Thirty-three if you count dead languages."

"Hah... dead being a relative term because... you're... dead— okay bad joke." I continued thumbing through the books. "But wow. No one would ever accuse *you* of wasting time."

"After the first hundred years, I knew I had to do something to make it all worthwhile. People these days chase after some form of eternal youth or immortality. Few actually know what it means."

"So if you could be the grand designer of life, what would be the perfect age to live and achieve as much as humanly possible?" I asked.

"It's all relative to the person and how they bide their time. Some people achieve more in ten years than others could in an entire lifetime. But if we're talking about someone active, willing to learn and explore—I'd say about two hundred years to acquire a decent grasp of all life has to offer."

"So you're way passed your prime." I giggled.

"I suppose so. That's another interesting thing... I'm always learning something new—meeting someone new. Aside from a few personality types and doppelgangers, most everyone today is completely different than those who lived even a hundred years ago." He stepped over to me. "I can safely say I've never met anyone quite like you before."

"What about Melena?"

"Good point. I've often compared you to her... but you two are very different as you are similar." He brought his hand to my face and gently caressed my cheek with his thumb.

It would have been easy for me to make a quip about him acting inappropriately, but the way he looked at me gave me pause... as if he were studying me like a long lost daughter. That in and of itself made me feel a little uncomfortable about thinking he was hot to begin with.

"Thank you." He smiled.

"Damn it. Stop that!" I smacked his hand away.

He looked down at the book I had picked up. "You're going to have to learn some Latin if you hope to be successful at your little paranormal investigating job."

"Patronizing much?"

"Don't take it the wrong way. I think it's adorable and completely appropriate for your skillset. Though limited, I could see you expanding to include more of what you were born to do."

"Which is?" I asked.

"Maintaining balance in the supernatural world."

"But you said things have been quiet...."

"I did. And now we have two unexplained murders on our hands. These things happen in cycles. Did your aunt share in your abilities?" he asked.

"No. She was a medium only... a psychic. My mother had the ability from what I understand, but she went a little nuts when I was a baby and became ultra-religious... as I told you the other night. I think my aunt knew more than she let on... perhaps to protect me from the truth. I would have appreciated a concrete answer about my mother, and I know there's more to it, but all I remember is the religious nut who freaked out at the mention of something paranormal. Someone who forced me to pray every night until she died."

"It sounds like your father changed her world in more ways than one."

"Probably. As much as I knew of my mother, I was told even less about my father. They wouldn't even tell me his name."

"Interesting."

"So help me out here," I said, lifting the book.

"This will take a while. You may just have to come back here more than once," he said with a wink.

"I don't know if this is you just being you, or if you're really hitting on me. Let me make this clear: yes, I think you're hot and alluring… in your own way, but I'm not going to sleep with you."

He continued to smile.

I tried to keep my expression serious. It would be easy to succumb to his wiles; he was educated, worldly, dashing… but also a vampire. "To make it easy on your ego—I would never hook up with a vampire… or any other supernatural creature for that matter."

"Racist."

"Oh no you didn't."

He laughed which caused me to laugh. "I'm just messing with you. Being romantically involved with a Tutorea is too dangerous."

"And you know this from personal experience."

"Yes," he said with a straight face. "*You're* very alluring. I don't say this to pay you a compliment. Many creatures will be drawn to you. In a way, it will make your job easier—you don't have to seek them out to see if they've been up to no good. When I first saw you, I felt compelled to approach you. And when you reacted the way you did, I realized why."

"Speaking of. You don't smell bad anymore. I suppose I noticed it was gone in the cab ride here."

"Really… interesting."

"I thought you said—"

"I know what I said." He looked concerned.

"Is something wrong?"

"I don't know yet."

His words left me uneasy which brought me full circle to another topic. "Lisbeth."

He looked at me. "What about Lisbeth?"

"What do you know?" I asked.

"I have no idea what you're talking about, my dear."

"You said you were surprised she had a boyfriend—why?"

"Fine." He closed the book he was thumbing through. "Remember how I told you I frequented certain clubs?"

"I guess."

"One of them in particular is a swingers club. I saw your friend there well before I knew who either of you were. When I approached you in the club and saw you speaking with her, I thought it best to keep my mouth shut about it."

"Why?"

"Well first of all, it's inappropriate to go up to someone and say, 'You may not remember me but I've seen you naked.'"

He had a point. "Okay so...."

"Well I told you it wasn't a big deal." He looked to the side.

"Oh come on, there's more, isn't there?" I folded my arms across my chest.

"Let's just say your friend is very bendy and accommodating."

"Okay, I'm not sure what you mean by that last part, but she told me she took gymnastics when she was younger."

"I mean accommodating in the sense that... she's unaffected by the size of things she allows to" —he looked to me again— "penetrate her. To be honest, it's quite impressive... how one so petite can—"

I closed my eyes and held up my hand. "Enough, I get the picture... though I'd really prefer not to. Let's just focus on the books, shall we?"

"You asked."

"Yes, and I regret asking now." I pulled out another book and perused the images. There was no way I'd understand the language, but at least I could get some semblance of what was going on by the pictures on the pages.

****

Rome spent the rest of the night reading me some of the entries in the books.

I pulled out my phone. "It's almost five. Ugh... I have to open tomorrow." I fell back into the couch.

"You can stay if you wish. I have plenty of rooms."

"Why do you even have a place this big? Suburban sprawl is horrible for the environment."

"Your concern for the planet is admirable... but I need my open space and large distances between me and the next person." He stood up. "If you'd like to go home, I'll pay for a taxi though I cannot escort you."

"Understandable." I looked around. "I suppose I could stay here. I'm curious to see more of this place."

"Well then," —he extended his hand— "join me and I shall give you a tour."

"Only if you promise to stop reading my mind every time you touch me."

"Promise."

I took his hand and he helped me up before leading me to the stairs to the second floor.

He opened a set of double doors. "You can use this room."

"Where do you sleep?"

"Careful, Onyx. When you ask things like that, I get mixed signals." I moved to say something but he held up his hand and laughed. "I am only kidding."

"It's a legit question. Do you use a coffin or something?"

"Not exactly. I'm in the master bedroom on the other side of the house. The windows are sealed with special shutters."

I was curious to see it, but I knew asking would give the wrong impression.

He smiled.

"What?"

"Nothing. You told me not to read your mind."

"Yeah but you clearly still are." I pulled my hand away.

"If you really want to see it, I won't think anything of it," he said.

I thought for a moment. "Okay."

He walked down the hall and I followed him to a larger set of double doors. He glanced over his shoulder and smiled at me before pushing them open.

Aside from a curtained bed in the middle, the rest of the room was like a smaller version of the house in regards to its museum-like status. "Seriously. Hoarder. You should see someone about that."

He laughed and moved behind me. "Was it what you expected?"

"Well I'm a little disappointed there's no coffin, but yeah, more or less."

"If you had a choice, would you sleep in a coffin, Goth girl?"

I could see what he was getting at. The idea is romanticized, but anyone who spent any time playing in a refrigerator box would know it would not be an ideal place to sleep in. I, for one, slept totally spread out like a starfish.

He lightly traced his fingers over my arm.

"What are you doing?" I asked.

"Tell me to stop."

I tried to clear my head of any and all thoughts. "Kiss my neck," I said.

He leaned down and kissed my neck. I reached around and ran my fingers through his hair.

"I want you to bite me."

He stopped. "What?"

"Do it."

"What are you doing, Onyx?"

Clearing my thoughts seemed to have worked. "I won't ask you again."

He slowly bit into my neck and drank a bit. The pain caused me to shriek, but like last time, a rush of endorphins kicked in.

"Stop," I said.

He stopped.

I turned and looked at him and sniffed. "Hm."

"What?"

"I don't smell anything. What does that mean?"

"Perhaps because you invited me to do it. Why was that, by the way?"

"That's for me to know and you to find out. Now, heal me."

He bit into his thumb and rubbed it over my neck, not once moving his gaze from mine. He leaned down and licked up the remainder of blood of my neck. Though the licking turned into full on kissing. My mind became flooded with thoughts of wanting him. "Say the words," he whispered.

"No. I want to go to bed." I purged the thoughts from my head and began walking away.

"Goodnight, Onyx."

"Goodnight, Rome," I said as I walked back to my room.

I woke up around 1 PM to my phone ringing. "What?"

"Did you want me to open the store?" asked Lisbeth.

"Ugh, shit. You don't have the keys. I'll be there in a few."

"Where are you?"

My eyes shot open. "Home."

"Okay… because I went there and you weren't there."

If she didn't sound so adorably cute all the time, I would have thought she was accusing me of something. "Um. I'm a pretty deep sleeper. I'll see you at the store."

I put on my boots and ran down the stairs.

There was no way I'd be able to walk from my location. The only option I had was calling a cab and I had about ten dollars in my pocket. I would end up having to grab cash from the store's register to pay for it once I got there.

As I approached the foyer, I saw an envelope on the table in the middle, with my name on it. It was obvious as to what it contained.

Onyx,

I know you'll probably leave it here, but I insist you take some money so you can at least get back home.

Yours, Romoalt

The way he signed his name looked like something you'd find on a historical document in a museum.

"Nope. Sorry, Rome. I just can't do it." I wasn't sure if he could hear me. I pulled out my phone again and called for a cab.

Chapter 13

Onyx

"So where were you *last* night?"

"I told you—home."

"Mmhmm, okay." Lisbeth clearly didn't believe me but she wasn't going to press either.

"You're late," Frank said as we walked in.

"I know, I'm sorry. I slept in... I'm allowed to do that on occasion, you know. Liz, can you open up the rest of the store? I want to check something online."

"Sure thing, boss."

I turned on the computer and searched for any news on the murder from last night. Two deaths and headlines were already talking about potential serial killers. "I'm sure the cops will love that one."

"Why's that?" Frank asked.

"They are saying it's a serial killer... and they wouldn't be wrong. It's just a term people jump on. Whatever is going on seems more supernatural than anything."

"Another ghost?"

"Nah. This thing had claws and used them—expertly. According to the books at Rome's house, there could be any number of creatures capable of this."

"So *that's* where you were."

"Ugh, don't say anything to Lisbeth, please."

"No problem. I'm going to spend time with the back TV... if you know what I mean," Frank said.

"Yeah. Please don't remind me."

Local news showed the club was closed pending investigation even though this particular incident occurred behind some other building. I could only imagine that was Elliot's doing based on the information Lisbeth provided to him.

Elliot

"They're saying 'serial killer' and we know the media frenzy that sort of thing generates," Nicki said.

"I know." I put my fingers to my temples and pressed down. "All we have to go on is the link to the club."

"What do we know about the owner?"

While pulling up his file I noticed a charge of harassment which was dropped about six months ago. "Looks like he's a rowdy one. Let's see, Erick Windheim, busted for assault in '09, possession last year; October. Also a dropped harassment charge six months ago—one of his former employees. Get this—her name is Alisha Hanson."

"I can smell the metal on the bars already," Nicki said as she stood up and grabbed her jacket. "Let's go question this son of a bitch."

****

Our first stop was the home address on file.

"Didn't know club ownership paid such a meager salary," Nicki said as she looked at the apartment building. "This place is...."

"Disgusting," I said.

Nicki pressed the buzzer on the outer door. "I'm going to need hand sanitizer after this."

"Who is it?" The words came from an older woman with a raspy voice.

"We're with the Philadelphia Police Department." Nicki looked at me for a moment. "There's been a complaint about the land lord. We just have a few questions."

"Nice," I mouthed to Nicki.

Seconds later, there was a buzz allowing us to enter the building.

We walked up to the third floor and knocked on the apartment door.

An older woman answered. Though by looking at her, she sounded much older than she really was. The apartment reeked of cigarettes as well. "So someone finally complained about the asshole who runs this dump."

"Sort of," Nicki said, actively looking past the woman. "May we come in?"

"Sure." The woman flung open the door and waved us in the apartment.

To be honest, I'd have much preferred to stay in the hall. "Are you the lessee to this apartment?"

"More or less."

"We had some questions about another possible resident… a Mr. Erick Windheim," I continued.

"He's my son. Why?"

"Just a formality," Nicki said as she wrote a few things down in her notepad. "Do you know where he is now?"

"He's at his club… Opening or something or other." She pulled out a cigarette and began to light up.

I looked at Nicki and arched a brow.

"Thank you, Ma'am," Nicki said as we both turned to leave.

"Wait, don't you want the details about this hell hole?"

"We'll be sending an inspector over to gather those details," Nick said in an effort to leave before the stench permeated our clothing.

"I guess we're going to the club," I said.

As we drove up, three men dressed in black were entering through the side door.

"What do you think that's about?" Nicki asked.

"Not sure."

"They don't look like salesmen... think we should call for backup?"

"I don't want to spook anyone. Let's just knock on the front door, shall we?" I asked as I got out of the car.

The same bouncer from Friday night answered the door. He narrowed his eyes at me. "What do you want?"

I showed him my badge this time. "Philadelphia PD, we're here to talk to your boss about the recent murders at this locations."

"Didn't he already give you his statement?" the bouncer asked.

"We're just doing a little follow-up. Not to be a jerk, but there have been two murders in the alley behind the building. Until it's solved, the media and police will be all over this place. We're just trying to make this easy for everyone involved." Being nice and polite was always first and foremost for me unless I was in a heated situation. By starting out with taking all the blame, people tended to open up and let their guard down.

"Come on in. Mr. Windheim has... *guests* right now, but I will let him know you're here." The bouncer walked off.

"*Guests*, huh," Nicki muttered. "I'm pretty sure at least one of those guys is packing heat." She got up and started to follow the bouncer.

I caught up to her. "What are you doing?" I asked in a hushed tone.

"Just wanting to see if I can hear a bit of the conversation."

"From here?"

"Well if there's arguing, we'll both know."

I narrowed my eyes at her for a moment.

She must have heard something I didn't, because just then, she pulled out her gun and rushed toward the door of the back office. "Drop it!"

I caught up to her just in time to see two of the three men in black holding guns pointed toward Mr. Windheim.

"Oh thank God you're here. Arrest these fools," he said.

"This is an active crime scene and there are more police on their way. I think you're going to want to drop those weapons," I said.

The two men set their guns down on the ground and held up their hands. The third man spoke up. "We have permits for those."

"We?" Nicki asked as she cuffed one of the men.

I holstered my weapon and cuffed the other one.

"Yes. These men are my private security. I'm a silent partner in this club and I came by to make sure business was going well, but I see the club has been closed again."

"And you are?" I asked.

"Marcus Donnelly."

It took me a moment but I recognized the name. He had his hands in various gambling establishments around town, and he claimed to be legit. Though his case wasn't one of mine, his name crossed my desk a few times.

"So Mr. Donnelly, why are you here?"

"Just coming to see why this club has been closed... again."

"Ah, so you're the man behind getting it reopened after the first murder."

He shrugged a bit and lifted his hands. "I'm just a guy looking after his investments."

"I'm sure you're aware there's been a second murder? I don't know what strings you pulled to get this place opened after the first one, but I highly doubt you'll have the same luck this time around." I uncuffed the man in front of me and nodded for Nicki to do the same. "We have some questions for Mr. Windheim if you don't mind."

"Not at all." He nodded to his guys and coolly walked out of the office, eyeing me while doing so.

"Does he normally threaten you?" I asked Mr. Windheim once Mr. Donnelly was gone.

"Only when he doesn't get his cut." He sat back at his desk. "What can I do you for, officer?"

"It's Detective. I'm Detective Stevens... this is Detective Alcott."

"I already gave my statement to some Longbear guy."

"Yes, but you seemed to have left out the part where you knew both of the victims."

He looked up at me then to Nicki, clearly nervous. "What makes you say that?"

I pulled out my phone and opened his file. "Alisha Hanson ring a bell?"

"She used to work for me." He loosened his tie a bit.

"Says here she reported that you were harassing her about six months ago."

"Those charges were dropped—what of it?"

"Well let's see... you lied to Sergeant Longbear about knowing her, you've had previous hostile encounters with someone who was found dead behind your club, what else?" I looked to Nicki.

"Oh yeah... and the other girl was a regular here," she added.

"Fine. I knew her. The other girl I didn't know. I think her name was Beverly or something. I've seen her around. Listen, lots of girls' approach me wanting to get comp'd—they offer... things... in order to... you know."

Nicki made a sound of disgust. "Pig."

"But I didn't kill nobody. Alisha and I dated for a short while. She caught me with someone else and broke up with me. I was only trying to get her back... then she goes and files this harassment report. Such bullshit."

"And now that's not a problem for you anymore," I said.

"Hey, like I said, those charges were dropped. I made it up to her. We were trying to smooth things over until she up and disappeared three months ago."

I stood up and handed him my card. "If you think of something else, let me know. It's a good thing your alibi was already verified for both nights in question."

"So what now?"

Nicki and I walked away without answering him.

"Hey! When am I getting my club back open?!" I heard him yell out before the door closed behind us.

****

"What a fucking bust," Nicki said, throwing her jacket on the desk chair. "We need a new plan."

"You should go talk to the M.E. and get more information about those wounds."

"And what are you going to do?"

"You're going to go undercover." I turned around to see Sergeant Longbear walking over to us.

"What?" I asked.

"You and your partner. I want you both at that club Friday night."

"The club's been closed until further notice," I said.

"Not anymore. Just got a call. The owner has more pull than I originally thought."

"Marcus Donnelly," I said.

"What?" he asked.

"We saw him today. He's one of the investors for the club and he showed up flashing his hired help."

"I believe narcotics is working a case on him. I'll let them know."

"Still want me to talk to the M.E.?" Nicki asked.

"Yes… looks like I need to go shopping," I said.

Chapter 14

Onyx

I didn't hear from Rome or Elliot until the following Friday, when the club had finally reopened.

Elliot showed up unexpectedly. "I need a favor."

"What?"

Lisbeth walked up to the counter with a hand pump bottle of lube and set it down. "We have a whole box of these in the back but no room for them anywhere."

I grabbed the bottle and examined it before extending it to Elliot. "Here. Compliments of the Mystery Box," I said in a snarky tone.

He sighed and shook his head. "I need your help with something."

I turned to Lisbeth. "I'll be back there in a sec. Just stock everything else."

"Right-o, boss."

"You don't talk to me for a week and now you come here wanting a favor?" I went back to filling out an order form in an effort to act dismissive.

Elliot stepped up to the counter and put his hands down. "Please."

"Come on! Ugh. Fine. What do you want?" I asked.

"Sergeant Longbear wants me to question people at Awakening. My partner says that's a bad idea since no one will talk to me... so the two of them came up with the brilliant idea of having me go undercover. Since you already know me and it's not like I can hide from you... I need your help."

I couldn't help but bust out laughing. "You want *me*... to help *you*... go undercover at a Goth club. This is rich. Wait, wait." I held up my hand and stared at him for a moment. Though I kept an expression of sarcastic amusement, I couldn't help but imagine how hot he'd look in rivet-wear. "Okay. I'll do it."

"Thank you—"

"One condition."

He sighed again. "What's that?"

"You keep me looped into the details of the case."

"I can't do that."

"Then I can't help you." I went back down to my order.

"Wait," —he rested his hand on top of mine which sent shockwaves through my body— "why do you want to be kept in the loop?"

"In case it is relevant to my night job." I swallowed and felt my heart rate increase.

"Fine. I will. But you cannot reveal the details of the case with anyone else... not even your friend Rome." The way he said Rome told me he had it out for him, though I couldn't imagine why. There was no way he'd know what Rome was.

I grabbed one of my business cards for the store and wrote down a name and address. "Go here, talk to this guy, and he'll set you up. If you want to be authentic, it's going to cost you a pretty penny."

"Alright." He took the card and gave me a once over before leaving.

"What was that about?" Lisbeth asked.

"Looks like our detective friend is going undercover at the club. George is going to have a field day."

Lisbeth gave me a questioning look.

"Let's go figure out this lube problem, shall we?"

Elliot

So this is the place. I debated going inside. Alternative Threads was a Goth store and it was obvious why Onyx sent me here.

"Let's get this over with," I said to myself as I walked inside.

The man behind the counter immediately took note of me. "Can I *help* you with something?"

Rather than get into the specifics, I handed the clerk the card Onyx gave me.

He laughed. "This is going to be fun."

"Why?"

"See this word here?" He lifted the card and pointed to the word "Enchilada" I hadn't noticed it.

"What does it mean?"

He smiled. "You'll see. By the way, my name is George. I'll be your clerk for this evening. If you'll follow me please." He led me to a dressing room and shoved me inside. "Don't move, I'll be back with items. Oh one more thing—take off your shirt."

"Why?"

"For the size, silly."

I rolled my eyes and grumbled as I took off my blazer and dress shirt before handing them to him.

"Fit," he said as he gave me a once over, "nice. I have just the thing. You look about a thirty-two pant size." He handed me my clothes and closed the door.

He came back after a few moments and tossed some clothing over the door.

"Do you have any piercings?"

"None you need to be concerned about," I said as I pulled some of the items off their hangers.

"Ooh. Onyx is just going to love that. Anyway, I was only asking in case I needed to hook you up with some jewelry. But... we sell *those* types of accessories too, if you're interested. Who would have thought a clean cut guy like you had—"

"Please. Stop talking," I said.

"Feisty. Georgie likie."

I heard him walk away. "You have some interesting friends, Onyx," I muttered as I looked at myself in the mirror.

"Aren't you going to model them for me?" I heard him say after a while.

I put back on my clothes and walked out of the dressing room. "No."

"I'm sorry. I can't let you leave."

"And why is that?"

"The code. Basically you're here for a makeover and I'm not allowed to let you leave until my work is done. You need this for tonight, right?"

I was growing impatient, but he was right. I had no idea what I was doing. "Yes, I do. Be quick about it." I handed him some of the items. "I'll just take these."

"Excellent choice, sir." He pulled off the tags and handed the items back to me. "Now get dressed. I'll ring you up and I have some things from my personal collection I'll be donating to the cause as well. Here's hoping you like eye liner."

"What?"

He walked away.

It was too late now. I went back into the dressing room and changed into the mock leather pants. The top had me even more confused than when I tried it on.

"You okay in there?"

"Not really."

"Open up, I'll help."

"Thanks, I'd rather not," I said.

"Ugh. You're Onyx's property, I wouldn't dream of hitting on you."

I swung open the door.

"Can I take back that last thing I said?" he asked as he eyed me up and down. He grabbed the top. "Yes, this one is complicated but it looks totes hot. We'll be doing a layered look, today."

Him switching between a very effeminate way of speaking, to a professional one was causing me to chuckle a bit.

The top was jersey knit with slashes through it and a layer of buckles and straps over it. He wasn't kidding: I looked quite good in it. "I have some accessories for you." He slapped leather cuffs on me as well as some silver rings. "These are mine, I'll be expecting them back." He handed me some mid-calf leather boots and pulled up a chair. "Sit. I need to do your makeup."

"That's really not necessary."

"The hell it isn't. Onyx wants a complete package so that's what she's going to get. Though I have no idea where she found you. You're more normal looking than most of *my* lovers."

I wasn't quite sure how to respond to that. Did he think I was her boyfriend? Did he even know I was a cop?

After he was done mussing my hair and smearing liner on my eyes, he faced me toward the mirror. "There. You are hot as hell. You should consider making this look a more permanent one."

Without saying a thing, I stared at myself in the mirror and handed him my credit card. *Is this what Onyx wants?*

"I shall be back, my good man."

After bagging up the rest of my things, he handed me my card and receipt, and sent me on my way. There was no way I'd go back to the station looking like this, and I felt weird approaching Onyx, so I went home and waited until the club opened for the evening.

Chapter 15

Onyx

"Oh my God, girl. That boy you sent over is *hot*. You're going to be very happy when you see him," George said through the phone.

I instantly felt nervous. "I don't think any of my old stuff is going to cut it. Can you swing by with a few things? I think I want to go all out in Victorian Goth."

"But you won't match your little toy."

"I don't care." All I knew was I needed to look good… irresistible even.

"I'll see what I can do… we have some new mock-bustle petticoats in. They don't even have the tags on them yet which means you can avoid a 'who wore it best' moment with those other bitches at the club."

"Little victories, I suppose. Actually… just meet me at the house. I still need a shower. Plus I need to grab a book for Rome's collection. He has quite a few books at his house."

"I knew it!" Lisbeth narrowed her eyes at me. "You were with that vampire guy huh?"

"What vampire guy? Oh God girl, don't tell me you're hanging with the douchebag wanna-be's," George said.

"No… ugh, I'll just see you at my house." I hung up the phone.

"Why didn't you tell me? It's not like I'd lecture you or anything… he's a hottie."

"It wasn't like that. I went over there for some research on whatever is going on. He let me stay over last Friday. His house is *huge*."

"Let's see... sexy, smart, rich... why are you messing with this cop anyway?" Lisbeth asked.

"I don't know. Maybe because he's different." I shrugged. "Also... I don't want to hook up with a vampire... gross." I thought it best to keep the happenings at Rome's house on the down low.

"I think it's hot."

"Then *you* hook up with him. I'd rather not get all necro."

"Ladies... please," Frank interjected. "Neither of them is worth your time."

"Aww, thanks Frank. That's like the sweetest thing you've ever said to me."

"No probs, toots."

"Lisbeth, I'm gonna need you to stay here while I get ready. Don't worry, I'll be back to give you time to go home and do the same."

"Okay, I guess. I still think you're wasting your time on this guy."

"Maybe. Now grab me one of those giant bottles of lube. I need to have something to give to George as payment."

****

George was waiting outside my house with a bag filled with goodies. I could see the tulle peeking out.

"Is that for me?" he asked, gesturing toward the bag in my hand.

"Maybe." I smiled and handed it over to him.

He gasped. "You know me so well. I was totally running out. Also, when did you get gallon sized lube bottles?"

"This morning. I think Lisbeth fucked up an order. Eh, at least we have some now in case customers ask." I opened the door and led George up to my room. "I need to look like a Goth queen tonight."

"Are you sleeping with this guy?"

"No…"

"What am I missing here? Is he someone you *want* to sleep with?"

Yes. "He just needed a favor from me… I can't really tell you what it is."

"Ooh, secrets. Oh, I brought you a surprise… something else that just arrived at the store. We only have three in stock, and now you own one of them." He produced a top hat which had black lace and ribbon hanging off the back and decorated with some black and red roses.

"Oh wow. I think you're going to have to come back with me to the store… what I gave you is not nearly enough for this."

He pulled out a burlesque bustled petticoat which had a train that nearly touched the floor.

"Yikes. That looks pricey."

"It is."

After my shower, George began helping me get dressed.

I slipped the petticoat over my boy-short panties before George laced up my corset.

"My goodness. You are going to look fierce tonight."

"I'm lucky I have plenty to work with already… even a pair of Victorian boots." I pulled them out and he grabbed them.

"How have I never seen these before?"

"I prefer my industrial grade combat boots, you know this. Anyway, I have to hurry and get back to the store. Lisbeth needs time to get ready too."

"Before you go." George pulled out a can of something and sprayed me.

"What the hell is that?" I coughed a bit and waved my hand in front of my face.

"Glitter… it's like a shimmery dust. It'll make you glow more than sparkle, trust me. This is the stuff go-go dancer's use at the gay club. It's magnificent."

I had to admit, I was looking pretty sexy.

"If I were to ever throw in the towel and diddle a female, you would be the one."

"George! You're making me blush." I giggled.

Back at the store, Lisbeth was floored by my appearance.

"There is no way I am going to be able to compete with that."

"It's not a competition. I only have eyes for one guy," I said.

"I'll meet you at the club tonight, is that okay?"

"Sure. See ya then." I sighed. "Frank. Do you think I'm stupid for liking this guy?"

"You know how I feel about cops, hon."

"Yeah but for a cop…."

"He ain't bad. One thing's for sure—don't go getting mixed up with that vampire business."

"Trust me. It couldn't be further from my mind," I said.

Though my house was within a few blocks of the store, the club was not. Generally, I'd take the bus and not think much of it… but that was before I decided to dress up like a burlesque dancer. One, I didn't feel like being gawked at by normies, and two, I didn't want to risk mussing up my clothes or makeup.

"Do you think it would be bad for me to use the register to pay for two cab trips in one week?"

"You're askin' me for advice about money? Come on," Frank said.

"It won't be more than ten bucks with tip. I can just put the money back Friday."

"Listen, girly. Don't put yourself out there for these guys. Make them come to you."

I chuckled a bit. "Sounds like something Aunt Belinda would say."

"Your aunt was a smart lady."

I collected my thoughts. "I'm not doing it for them. I'm doing this for me and to make sure no more girls get hurt."

"Then there ya go."

After calling a cab, I grabbed my keys and went outside. Frank meant well, but a part of me was actually doing this to impress Elliot.

****

I arrived at the club just in time to see a line out the door. It seemed the murders surrounding this place increased its street cred. *How depressing is that?*

The bouncer caught me as I headed to the back of the line.

"Oh no, missy, you're up here."

"Since when do I get VIP treatment?" I asked.

"Since you're the best looking thing to cross my path tonight."

I giggled. It was rare for me to get an outright compliment. "Why thank you, kind sir," I said as I walked into the club.

It was wall to wall packed and the bar had no room. *Guess I'm not drinking tonight.* The amount of people concerned me. Finding whomever was behind this would prove difficult with a crowd such as this one.

"You're finally here! Can you believe this crowd?" Lisbeth said as she approached me. I smiled at her attempt to copy my look. It actually complimented mine more than anything.

"I know, it's crazy. So have you seen you-know-who yet?"

"Nah. Hey listen, I got us a private booth in the back. I think the owner still regrets firing me and he's been extra nice to me since I told him I broke up with Dave."

"Nice. I guess I *will* be drinking tonight." I followed her toward the back booths and sat down. They were up a few steps

127

which allowed for a decent view of the dance floor, entrance, and bar.

"So what do you want to drink?" Lisbeth asked.

"I think tonight is going to be a vodka night. Did you get a hookup for a bottle too?"

She nodded and smiled.

"Then make it top shelf, lady."

She caught one of the waitresses and whispered something in her ear. The waitress nodded and walked away. As I followed her path with my eyes, I saw Rome. He immediately looked up at me and smiled as he approached.

He took my hand and whispered in my ear. "You look good enough to—"

"Don't say it… and thank you," I whispered back.

"How did you manage to swing a table?"

I'm pretty sure it was a low blow reference to my financial situation. Maybe he was upset I didn't take his money before. "It was all Lisbeth. By the way, she has a crush on you. You should get to know her better."

He pulled away and looked me in the eye. His expression grew a little dark, almost like the mere suggestion was insulting.

"What?"

"Nothing." He glanced over to Lisbeth who gave him an innocent smile. He smiled back though it seemed forced. Then again, I could have been reading into it. He looked back at me. "I saw your detective friend at the front door."

"Really?" I asked. It came out more excited than I had planned.

"He wasn't alone." Just a hint of a wicked smile crept on his face.

"Whatever. It's probably his partner or something… the werewolf."

"Ah yes. Formally meeting her should be interesting indeed," he said. He ran his fingers over the brim of my hat. "Nice hat."

"Thanks," I said. I looked into the crowd once more and saw George. He wasn't looking my direction so I excused myself from Rome's side and headed over to him.

"George!" I called out as I weaved my way through the dense crowd.

"Oh thank God! I was beginning to think I'd be stuck with the peasants. Lisbeth texted me and said she had a table."

"She sure does. This way." I turned to head back toward the booth and nearly ran into Elliot. George wasn't kidding. He was drop dead gorgeous. It took every ounce of my willpower not to let my jaw drop open. It was a little easier when I took note of his partner standing right next to him.

His lips curled ever so slightly as he eyed me up and down. I assumed he was pleased until he opened his mouth. "I'd ask you kindly not to tell anyone who I am… or Detective Alcott."

Detective Alcott arched her brow at me. As far as attire went, she didn't do half bad. Though she had nothing on me. "Fine. We have a table in the back. Might as well hang out with us so you don't get yourself in trouble."

"No, thank you. We're going to stay near the entrance and watch," said Elliot.

"Okay. Just so you know, the booth we have has a great vantage point. Your loss." I started to walk away and he stopped me.

"Fine. Just let your friends know to keep their mouth shut or I'll arrest them. All of them… and you."

"Wow, okay, calm the hell down. I'm trying to help *you* out, remember?"

Detective Alcott and Elliot both followed me back to the booth. Rome seemed surprised at the new arrival before his earlier wicked grin morphed into a full blown one. "What a lovely surprise, Det—"

I shot him a look then shook my head.

"Ah, I see." He put his finger to his lips in a "shh" gesture. "So this must be your… friend," he said to Elliot, referring to Detective Alcott.

"It would help if I had another name to call her," I said.

"Nicki. My name is Nicki," she said as she inched closer to Elliot.

Rome was spot on about the scents. I could barely catch a whiff of anything other than perfume coming from Nicki. It was a relief all things considered. At least now I could be nicer to her. "We have a bottle coming, but I know you two probably... can't... drink?"

Elliot shook his head.

"More for me," I said with a smile.

"There are so many hot guys here tonight," George whispered in my ear.

"Notoriety brings out all the crazies. And we both know you can't be hot and sane at the same time," I whispered back.

"Says you," Rome said.

Elliot seemed confused at what he observed was a one-sided discussion.

I shot Rome another look.

Nicki scowled at Rome a bit before looking at me.

"Care to dance?" I asked George.

"Oh yes, hunty. The best way to nab man meat is to bump against it on the dance floor, let's go."

I giggled as he grabbed my hand and led me toward the crowd. There was barely enough room to move but we made it happen.

"So was that the wanna-be vampire guy?" George asked.

"Yes."

"You're right, he's too good looking for that crowd."

"He is indeed." I looked back over to the booth to see everyone watching George and I dance. *Shouldn't you be watching the rest of the crowd, officer?*

Of all the guys here though, there's no one I'd rather dance with than George. He was spectacular, and spent his earlier years as a professional go-go dancer at some of the local gay clubs.

As we danced I caught a scent. It was exactly like the scent in the alleyway. I immediately grew alert and started looking around. It was faint, but it was there. In order to mask attempts at recon, I led George to various spots on the floor, trying to catch a strong scent.

"What is it?" George asked, probably noting the look of concern on my face.

"Nothing. I just… never mind."

The only area we hadn't gotten close to yet was the bar so I led him back in that direction. Finally, the scent grew stronger. Whoever it was had to be standing at the bar. As I looked over the crowd, trying to eliminate those I knew to be regulars, no one stood out.

"Who are you looking for?"

"No one," I immediately responded, trying to deflect any further questions. I looked up at the booth and saw the same four looking back at me, except this time, Rome was walking toward us. Elliot put his hand on Rome's shoulder to stop him, though I couldn't imagine why. The scent was starting to drift away. "Give me a sec, George."

"Everything okay?"

"It will be." I flashed him my smile and walked around the club trying to pick up the scent again.

Whoever it was had either left or moved very quickly, to another part of the club. My nose was getting overloaded with the scents of sweat, perfume and cologne.

"Damn it." I looked back over to the booth and saw Rome finally walking toward me. "About damn time."

"Did you see something?"

"More like smelled something. It was the same scent from last week. I know what it is but I can't think of the name… it's like burning rock."

"Sulfur?"

"Yes! That's it exactly. I hadn't smelled it since ninth grade science class."

His expression turned grim. "That's not good. Not good at all."

"Why?"

"If you're smelling sulfur, it means it's a demon attacking these girls."

"Seriously? Like a demon from hell?"

"I use demon in the non-religious sense. It's just another type of supernatural creature which walks among us though many of them have been eliminated over the years. Remember when I said some creatures cannot be managed?"

I nodded.

"Well a demon is one of them. Where did it go?"

"I don't know. I lost the scent, I thought you'd be faster."

"Your friend stopped me—asked me where I was off to. Apparently, he still doesn't trust me," Rome said as he glanced up to the booth.

"So what do we do? How do we get rid of it...? I don't remember reading about demons in the books you showed me. I only know about exorcisms."

"That's because we didn't get that far. As for getting rid of it... depends on what kind of demon it is."

He took my hand and led me around the club, allowing me to try and catch the scent once more.

"Interesting."

"What?" I paused and looked at him.

"You're jealous of Detective Alcott."

"Would you fucking stop that already?"

"I'm sorry, it was right there and too strong to ignore."

"I'm not jealous... she's just a stinky werewolf," I said. Finally, I caught the scent again, though it was very faint. "I smell it. It's still here at least... there's just no way I can find it in this crowd." When I looked up again, we were near the back booths. As I stepped passed each one, I slyly leaned over trying to catch a whiff. The scent remained faint, at least in this area. We got back to our booth. "Did you guys see anyone come this way?"

"Why?" Elliot asked.

"Just curious."

"Just people going to the bathroom," Nicki said.

I walked toward the bathrooms and Elliot stopped me. "Is this related to what's going on?" he asked.

"No. I'm just looking for someone." There was no way I could explain to him that we were all chasing down a demon. The only way out of this place was the front and side door, which meant whoever this demon was, would have to walk by the booth in order to leave. Rather than keep Elliot on my case, I sat down.

He sat next to me with Nicki on his other side.

The waitress finally came with a bottle of top shelf vodka and some mixers. "Finally," I said.

"Ooh, yay, booze." George came back over and poured himself a shot. "Sorry to drink and run, but I just met the hottest guy. See ya tomorrow." He blew me a kiss before running off.

"If only it were that lucky for me," Lisbeth said.

"Aww." I wrapped my arm around her shoulder and held her close to me. The scent was getting weaker which began to worry me. I still had questions for Rome but I couldn't ask them in front of Elliot and Nicki. An idea popped into my head. I reached under the table and grabbed Rome's hand. He seemed pleased for a moment before he realized what I was doing. *"Is there any way a creature could mask their scent from me?"*

He shook his head.

"Well shit," I said.

"Well shit what?" Nicki asked.

"Nothing. I guess my friend bailed after all." I moved to pull back my hand but Rome held on tight, giving me a gentle caress with his thumb before finally letting me go. I scowled at him; he met it with a smile.

Elliot kept looking between the two of us, clearly suspicious.

To keep his mind elsewhere, I "accidentally" bumped my leg against Elliot's under the table.

He looked at me for a moment, his expression calmed a bit and soon after, I felt his fingertips trace over my thigh. I bit my lip as he gently touched me. He kept his eyes locked on mine while he did it which made it that much harder to control my racing heart. There was no doubt... I wanted him.

I reached my hand over to his thigh and mimicked his movements. He reacted enough for only me to notice, though I'm pretty sure the two other creatures at the table would instantly recognize the increased vascular activity. I was curious as to how far he'd let me go as I trailed my fingers further up the inside of his thigh. The feel of the material of his pants also triggered something within me. Right now he was the best of both worlds: a clean cut guy playing bad boy. He allowed me to continue on my little adventure or so it would seem.

"I think I'm going to check the hall in the back," I said as I looked at Elliot to get up.

"Mind if I join you?" Elliot asked.

I looked at Nicki then back to Elliot. "Not at all."

Nicki grumbled as she slid back into the booth after moving to let Elliot out.

Elliot and I walked down the hall. I saw the door to the janitor's closet which was labeled "Private," and opened the door.

"How did you know it was open?" Elliot asked.

"All the regulars know this room is open."

Elliot closed the door behind him and stepped toward me, causing me to back into one of the metal shelves. He looked at me for a moment before leaning into kiss me.

I jerked my head to the side. "I don't want to ruin my makeup. Though if you're willing, you can use that mouth elsewhere."

He leaned down and began kissing my neck. He was much softer and gentler than the way Rome did it. Perhaps I preferred it light and easy after all….

He reached into his back pocket and pulled out his handcuffs. *Perhaps not.*

The expression on his face was unfaltering as he cuffed my wrists around a metal bar above my head before moving down to his knees, sliding off my boy short panties in the same action.

As he kissed my inner thigh, he pushed my bustle skirt further up. I propped up my leg on one of the adjacent shelves to give him easier access. He immediately dove right in and began darting his tongue in and out of my wet opening before swirling it around my clit.

I gasped and moaned at the sensation. My wrists being bound filled me with regret that I couldn't run my fingers through his hair.

He moved my other leg over his shoulder and gripped his hands under my ass, lifting me up. His doing all the work allowed me to fall into ecstasy much easier. It felt amazing as I was doing everything in my power to keep from coming too soon, even though we were pressed for time. But if his intention was to get me off as quick as possible, he was succeeding like a pro.

Finally, I felt a rush through my body as I came while moaning uncontrollably. He set me down and grabbed a set of keys before unlocking the cuffs.

I couldn't help but wrap my arms around his neck and pull him in for a kiss.

He broke it. "I thought you didn't want to ruin your makeup?"

"Fuck it. I want to taste me on your lips." I resumed kissing him and he wrapped his hands under my ass again, lifting me up. I could feel his hardness between my legs through his pants. "Do you have a condom?" I asked.

"No. Unfortunately, I do not."

I looked at his lips and smiled. "You're lucky. I guess this lip stain doesn't smear."

He set me down again and helped me slip on my panties. He gave my stomach a kiss before standing straight up. "You taste amazing," he whispered seductively in my ear.

"Stop," I said with a whisper. "You're making it difficult for me not to throw you down on the ground and have my way with you, detective."

"Next time," he said.

We stepped out of the closet and walked back to the booth, sitting opposite each other while Rome and Nicki slid in closer to Lisbeth.

Rome smiled at me and I figured I'd taunt him with images of what happened, so I grabbed his hand under the table.

"Bad girl," he whispered in my ear.

Nicki, being a werewolf, had probably already guessed what had happened within seconds of us returning. Even if she didn't have keen predatory abilities, the look on her face made it quite obvious as to how she felt to begin with.

I guided Rome's hand between my legs and into my boy shorts so he could feel the wetness. He took the opportunity to slide a finger in before coyly and casually sticking it in his mouth. He closed his eyes a moment as if he were relishing in the taste.

Elliot was looking to the crowd and thankfully didn't witness my interaction with Rome.

Just then, a rush of the demon's scent flooded my nostrils which caused me to look up. A small group of men walked past the table. I couldn't be sure who it was, though one thing was for certain: I couldn't let them leave my sight.

I quickly looked to Rome then back to the small group of guys.

Rome nodded and followed me out of the booth.

Elliot seemed jarred from his daze. "Where are you off to?"

"I think I see my friend."

Rome looked to be at a loss when one of the men broke off from the other two. I rushed to his side to try and catch the scent of the two men in front of him. "It's not these two. It has to be the other guy. Did you see his face?" I asked.

"No. Did you?"

"No. He was well hidden next to those other guys. Shit. Though I still have his scent. Let's go." I followed in the direction I saw the man walk off to, trying to keep on him like a bloodhound.

"I have to admit, that image of you with your detective friend is quite the turn on," Rome said.

"That's why I showed you."

"When I got up, I touched our werewolf friend. I'm sorry about saying you were jealous of her earlier."

"Why?"

"Because when I touched her, I saw all sorts of violent imagery involving you. It's quite amazing how she's able to keep it in check, but she is very jealous of you. I'd watch out."

"She knows she can't break the rules."

"She's a woman… this has nothing to do with the beast within," he said with a chuckle.

"Fuck. It's gone again. He's probably here to scout out another victim. We can't let him."

Rome stood in front of me and brought his hands to my shoulders. "Close your eyes and clear your mind. Try to eliminate the other scents in the room and focus. I'll know if you're not following my instructions."

I rolled my eyes before closing them and doing as told. The scent was still there, in the background, though this time, I was able to focus on it. "I have it."

"Good. Keep your eyes closed and trust me, I'll lead you. Just tell me where to go."

"Straight. No wait… to the right. Wait stop." I turned around. "It's behind me now."

"It's alright. It seems he's making his way around the room. Just keep following it."

We continued walking and the scent grew stronger. Finally we stopped.

"Do you still smell it?"

I nodded.

"Really? Open your eyes."

I opened my eyes and we were facing the booth. Nicki and Elliot were staring at us like we were insane. Lisbeth was gone. "Where is Lisbeth?" I asked Elliot.

"Someone asked her to dance. She seemed to know them so we didn't pay it any mind."

"You saw him?!"

"Yes. Why?" Elliot looked concerned.

"He's the guy! He has Lisbeth. Where did they go?"

Nicki and Elliot immediately got up. "To the dance floor."

I turned around and scanned the dance floor and saw nothing. The only other place they could have gone without me still being able to see them, was the side door. I ran down to it and pushed through the door. There was a bouncer standing just outside. "Did you see two people leave just now? A man and a woman. She's about five foot tall, super petite with long black hair."

"Yes," the bouncer said while gesturing with his thumb, "they were headed further down the alley."

"Thanks," I said as I took off running.

Rome, Elliot and Nicki caught up to me. "Where did he take her?" Elliot asked.

"I'm not sure. The bouncer said they came—" I looked down a side alley just in time to see a large winged man lift an unconscious Lisbeth off into the night sky. "Lisbeth!" I screamed her name as I ran toward them. Within seconds they were both gone.

Elliot ran up to me with his gun out. "What in the hell was that?"

I looked at Rome, then Nicki, then finally back to Elliot. "Do you want the long version or the quick version so we can get started on finding a way to get my best friend back before she gets slashed to pieces?" I looked back out to the night sky and felt an overwhelming feeling of fear and despair.

Elliot looked to Rome. "Well someone needs to explain to me what we're dealing with."

"Not here," Rome said.

Rome suggested we all go back to his place to discuss things further. Not a word was spoken the entire car ride there.

Again, I found myself in Rome's house which came off more like a museum than anything.

"I'd offer you something to drink but I'm afraid I don't have much."

Of course he wouldn't. Being a vampire, Rome wouldn't stock up on anything except tap water; I was surprised he had a fridge at all.

Oddly enough, Nicki seemed less surprised by the statement. Though Rome was aware of Nicki being a werewolf, it seemed unlikely Nicki would know what Rome was by any other means than figuring it out on her own. For anyone with their foot in the supernatural world, it wouldn't be hard to take a wild guess.

Elliot was still trying to rationalize what he had just seen. Believing in ghosts was one thing, but seeing a demon was another thing altogether.

"It was some elaborate setup—a trick. Killers have been known to do worse," Elliot said.

"If only it were that simple. I think you should sit, detective," Rome replied.

"I'd rather stand, thank you."

Nicki sat down. It was clear from our first encounter, she didn't know what I was. The look on her face told me she might have some idea of what we were up against. She looked to Rome.

"What took my best friend?" I finally asked, wanting clarification.

"That, my dear, looked to be an incubus. Based on the type of murders which have occurred so far, I'm surprised at myself for not recognizing it sooner."

"A what?" Elliot asked.

"An incubus. It's a type of demon—"

"This is ridiculous. I should be gathering a squad for a rescue, and talking to Sergeant Longbear about initiating a manhunt for... whatever that was." Elliot moved to walk away.

"Elliot, stop." Nicki looked up at him. "He's telling the truth."

"And what? You're the expert because of your last job?"

At any point, Nicki could have announced to Elliot what the rest of us knew to be true. I couldn't imagine she'd have any idea that Rome and I both knew what she was and based on her next statement and hesitance to make it, my assumptions were founded. "Yes. I told you, I've seen some unexplainable things during my time in that unit."

"So a demon. Do we need a priest now?" Elliot asked. He was three against one in the fact department, yet he was still being sarcastic and disbelieving. Perhaps it was a self-defense mechanism of sort. I've been known to react the same way when confronted with unusual situations.

"Not exactly. Though you can rest assure Lisbeth will be safe... at least for a week."

"How?" I asked.

"Incubi's sole purpose is to breed. My guess is those other two women weren't sufficient enough hosts for his spawn."

"How do you know all this?" Elliot asked.

Nicki looked to Rome, obviously thinking the same thing. If Nicki was playing the same game of secrets as the rest of us, she had to know Rome wouldn't outright reveal himself, not even to her.

"I've studied them," Rome said.

"I thought you were a history buff. Last I checked, demons weren't a part of factual history."

"History buff?" Rome glanced over to me.

"Does it matter what he is? He's trying to help—just listen to him," I said.

"Trust me on this, detective. I want Lisbeth back more than you want to solve your case."

"You make me sound so heartless," Elliot said.

At least I knew Rome was on my side.

"Elliot..."

He lifted his eyes to me.

"There are things in this world which exist and have existed for eons. Things the average human doesn't know about."

"Average human? What is this?"

"Elliot, think of every horror story you read as a child, every legend you've heard—hell, every movie you've watched. It's all real—all of it. I'm still learning about it myself."

"Onyx, don't—"

"He's in way too deep, Rome. It's not like we can all skip out of here going 'ha ha, it's all a joke, see ya next Friday for an encore.'" I turned back to Elliot. "Apparently I'm what's called a

Tutorea. I have the ability to sniff out supernatural creatures—literally."

Nicki immediately looked at me with her jaw dropped. I wasn't quite sure what realizations she could possibly be having. Still, I didn't want to out her to her partner.

"I can't tell you everything... but I can tell you about me. Certain things, people, have distinct scents. Some groups all smell the same. For example, the demon tonight smelled like sulfur. If we ran into another demon, he'd smell like sulfur too."

Elliot finally sat down. I couldn't tell if he believed me or was still absorbing all of this new information.

"It's no big deal, really. It's like a scientist discovering a new species in the ocean. It's already there... you're just now finding out about it."

Rome started laughing.

Nicki still looked shocked.

Elliot glanced to Rome then back to me. "So what else is there?"

"That's the thing. There are rules. Technically, I shouldn't have told you what I just did, but I figure if I keep it light—the consequences won't be as severe. Part of keeping it light means there are certain things I can't talk about. First, it's not my place, and second, I don't know all of what there is yet. If you hang out with me long enough, you'll eventually figure it out or see it for yourself."

"I don't understand. What are these rules?"

"Well every society has its laws and rules. *This* society has them too. To name a few: we can't disclose anything about ourselves to humans—outsiders, if you will, we can't harm humans or interfere with their lives—"

"Wait, then how does he know?" Elliot looked back over to Rome. "What are you?"

"See, you can't ask questions like that."

"Why not?" Elliot glanced over to me before turning back to Rome. "Well, answer me?"

"I'm... a person," Rome said.

"Elliot. Ugh, just—please. I can't tell you anything else, but you have to work with us on getting Lisbeth back and not ask any more questions. Like I said, in time, all will be revealed." Rome was shaking his head in disappointment. I continued, "It's inevitable at this point."

Rome looked to the window. "I need my beauty sleep" — which was probably code for "daylight"— "you should probably head home. I'll research some of the books I have on the topic. You're free to stay here if you'd like," Rome said to me.

"I'll take her home," Elliot immediately responded.

"Very well then."

"We can see ourselves out," I said, reassuring Rome.

Chapter 16

Elliot

Demons. Every minute I spent in Onyx's world, the more ridiculous everything seemed. Even with Nicki assuring me it was all truth, I couldn't help but doubt everything I had seen up until now.

Nicki's apartment was further away than Onyx's, but I chose to drop her off first. Despite what went down earlier, Onyx and I needed to talk.

"I guess I'll see you later today," Onyx said as she moved to get out of the car.

"Wait."

"I told you. I can't tell you anything more than I already have."

"That's not what I want to discuss… the club."

"What about it?"

"Want to tell me why you—"

"Why I… what? Let you go down on me? Was it something you *didn't* want?" she asked.

Oh, I wanted it. In fact, I wanted more than just that. Even the surreal events of the evening couldn't break my ever-growing feelings for her.

In an unexpected move, she leaned over and kissed me. "You're welcome to stay… I have a guest room."

Was she telling me that for my benefit? "I'm going to head home and shower then go straight to the station."

"You look more exhausted than I feel," she said.

"I'm going to do everything in my power to get Lisbeth back."

"Thank you for believing me and helping."

"I'm not quite sure I believe it... or maybe I do and it's all still sinking in." I held my hands to my head. "Either way, this has been a long night. You should get some sleep."

She nodded and got out of the car. I waited and watched as she walked back into her house. More than anything, I wanted to follow her in and stay; even just to hold her until she fell asleep. The rational part of my brain was taking over, I needed to keep my head in the game if I wanted to be useful to both her and Lisbeth.

Lisbeth

Wherever I was, it was cozy and soft. I opened my eyes and looked around to see myself resting on top of fur and velvet throws. A roaring fire opposite the room showed the silhouette of a very tall man standing before it. Instantly, he took note of my movements and turned around.

"Hello?" I asked.

"Hello, Lisbeth."

"Where am I? How do you know my name?"

He didn't give an immediate answer which worried me. This was the man who had taken me. The last thing I remember was seeing him at Awakening and recognizing him from yet another club; Echoes, a swingers club. The encounter was brief and I was drunk. Even after meeting him again tonight, I'd almost forgotten how unbelievably gorgeous he was. *Gorgeous equals crazy.* My weakness for hot guys was starting to take its toll on me, especially after Dave.

While remaining silent, he began crawling toward me on the bed. As he got closer to the lamplight, I could make out more of his body and face.

"Why did you take me?" I asked.

He looked at me as if he were studying my face. "You will find out soon enough."

Acknowledgements

Thanks to all my friends and family for the help and support while working on this project. I'd like to thank Marco for keeping my social media clean and up to date and my Aunt Su for recommending some really awesome and helpful resources.

For additional volumes, check out my website www.bettinabusiello.com!

Printed in Great Britain
by Amazon